Death Stalks the Range

Brett Rider

SAGEBRUSH
Large Print Westerns

First published in Great Britain by Harrap
First published in the United States by MaCrae-Smith

First Isis Edition
published 2019
by arrangement with
Golden West Literary Agency

A catalogue record for this book is available
from the British Library.

ISBN 978–1–78541–687–3 (pb)

Published by
F. A. Thorpe (Publishing)
Anstey, Leicestershire

Set by Words & Graphics Ltd.
Anstey, Leicestershire
Printed and bound in Great Britain by
T. J. International Ltd., Padstow, Cornwall

This book is printed on acid-free paper

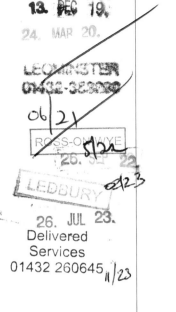
DE[A]

Rand Kenz[...]
through the [...]
held by liv[...]
reached Palo[...]
appeal to the [...]
week — mur[...]
of the troubl[...]
bullets are s[...]
where to be[...]
mystery. He [...]
Pinto whose [...]
an attempt i[...]
he's sure he'[...]
double dealir[...]
unravel many[...]
he can unma[...]

Please return/renew this item by the last date shown

SPECIAL MESSAGE TO READERS

AFFECTIONATELY
INSCRIBED TO
MY NIECE
Muriel Gooden

CHAPTER
ONE

The paint haze of dust appeared on the hillside where the road dropped in a long double loop to the town on the flats. Sam Bleeker watched it from the doorway of his store, a hand lifted over his eyes to break the glare of the sun now low to the peaks beyond. He spoke to his clerk, somewhere in the dim interior behind him. "She's evening, Fred." Sam Bleeker paused, added with a hint of surprise, "Looks like old Sundown is making up for lost time. He's sure burnin' dust."

Fred appeared at his shoulder, a thin, hollow-chested youth with unkempt black hair and pale, shifty eyes. He invaded an old-fashioned brass telescope at the distant stage. "Sundown ain't drivin'," he announced excitedly. "It's a girl — there can on the front seat. Don't see nothin' at old Sundown."

Sam snatched the telescope from the clerk's hands. "By grab!" Astonishment put a crackle in his voice. "That's Benita Ellison settin' there — and no sign of Sundown Skaggs."

Another pair of eyes had spotted the wildly careening stage, the very keen and understanding eyes of old Abel Gregg. He stood in the entrance of his cavernous livery barn. Concern stamped his leathery, desert-burned fact

1

with harsh lines of shock and alarm. His look shifted to a man who rode up on a black-maned buckskin horse. Abel had never seen him before, but this thing called for quick action. Hurry sharpened the usual drawl in his voice. "Son — there's somethin' wrong with the stage yonder. Looks like there's a gal handlin' the lines and she's let them mules get away with her."

The stranger swung his horse, sent his gaze into the blinding shimmer of the setting sun. "You've got good eyes, mister," he said. "Eyes like an eagle, but you're right at that. It's a girl tooling that team down the grade."

"Get a move on," Abel said. "There's like to be a bad spill. Them damn mules of Sundown's is sure on the stampede with the stage." Despite his anxiety he was conscious of an indefinable something about the tall young man on the buckskin horse, a quality of quiet resoluteness, a lean, hard body lightly poised in the saddle, a calm, forthright look of blue eyes set in a face that would have been stern save for the hint of humor in the wide, firm-lipped mouth.

"I'm on my way," the stranger said laconically. The buckskin dug in hoofs, was gone like an arrow sped from taut bowstring.

Abel watched, a hint of approval in his eyes. The man could ride, and the horse could run. He knew men, and he knew horses. This stranger and the buckskin under him made a pair that gripped his imagination.

His gaze shifted ahead to the distant stage rocking down the steep grade. He stifled a groan as the vehicle careened from view around a perilous hairpin turn. He would, at that moment, have given everything he possessed to be where that girl was sitting, the lines gripped in his own experienced hands. Abel had a fondness for Benita Ellison. She was the only child of the man who had been his best friend. An orphan now, for within the week, big, kindly Ben Ellison had been found mysteriously dead, a charge of buckshot in his back.

The runaway mules with the big stage lurching crazily at their heels reappeared in the long stretch that made a bee line down to the flats. A relieved grunt exploded from Abel. He turned quickly into the dim depths of the big barn. He ran with a noticeable limp, mememto of an old arrow wound in his thigh.

A graying, paunchy Mexican stable hand was cinching a saddle on a fast-looking red roan mare. Abel snatched a bridle from a peg and crammed the bit between the mare's teeth. She rolled wicked eyes at him, laid back her ears in indignant protest at his haste.

Abel's hard, wiry body lifted with the lightness of a feather into the saddle. He gave the Mexican a brief look. For all his anxiety his voice was quiet, crisply commanding. "Get running for Doc Smeed's office, Pablo," he said. "Tell him it looks like he'll be needed when the stage gets in."

"I go queek," Pablo answered. In his youth he had ridden with revolutionists below the border and crowding excitement made a deep livid crease of the machete scar across saddle-colored cheek. "*Por Dios!* She be keel . . . our leetle señorita! *Ay Dios mio!*" Muttering exclamations of grief and dismay, the

Mexican started on a heavy-footed run down the street. Dust was already bannering up from the red roan mare's hammering hoofs.

The road came down from the hills in a precipitous drop before it reached in a straightaway across the flats toward the little cowtown that lay inside the bend of the sluggish Rio Palo Pinto. It was imperative to bring the stampeding mules under control before their headlong flight carried them and the big Concord stage rocking at their flying heels into the sandy shallows of the crossing.

The thought of the resulting disaster sent a wave of gooseflesh over Abel Gregg. It was going to take quick thinking to bring that stage to a halt before it hurtled to its doom in the quicksands of the Palo Pinto.

It became apparent that the rider of the buckskin horse, a scant quarter of a mile in the lead, shared Abel's apprehensions. He suddenly left the road, made a sharp circle that reversed his direction and brought him alongside the foam-leathered mules. It was a feat that drew an approving grunt from Abel. The least error in timing would have sent the superbly running buckskin cannonading against the spinning wheels of the careening stage.

A strong brown hand grasped the bridle of the near mule of the lead team, and in response to the firm pressure, and the crowding shoulders of the buckskin horse, the mule pushed against it make. In a moment the runaways were swinging across the sunbaked mud flats in shortening circles, buckskin horse and rider clinging like burrs to the side of the lead team. The

4

going was too heavy for even insensate panic to withstand. The spinning wheels sank deep into sand that dragged the weary mules to a standstill. Heads hanging dejectedly, sweat-lathered sides heaving, they stood meek as lambs, the devil gone out of them.

Abel Gregg loped up on his roan mare. He threw the buckskin's rider a brief nod. "Smart work, son," he said laconically. His look went to the girl on the high box seat. She sat tense and straight, leather lines still bunched in clenched hands, her face pale under wind-whipped dark hair framed against the back-slanted white Stetson. Abel said mildly, "Hello, Benita." His eyes though, were anxious, questioning.

The lines dropped from her hands and she stared back at him, looked briefly at the tall young man watching from his saddle. "Abel —" It was obvious she was fighting desperately to keep the tremble cut of her low voice. "Sundown's been shot —" Her gesture sent the grizzled liveryman leaping for a look inside the stage.

The girl got up unsteadily from the seat. She was of medium height, slim and trim in short black skirt and jacket. An attractive, capable girl, with dark eyes that gave out topaz lights against the setting sun when she turned her head in another look at the buckskin's rider. He sensed taut nerves, a bodily weariness in her as she swayed there, a hand seeking blindly for the seat at her back.

In an instant the man was down from his saddle and pressing close to the wheel. "Here," he said. His two hands reached up to her, and suddenly she was down

5

on the ground, the weight of her against his shoulder, his supporting arm around her.

Only for an instant, then she drew back with a little shake of her head as if annoyed at her momentary weakness. "I'm — I'm all right," she said, and she added with an upward lift of her eyes into his, "You are very strong."

Before he could respond they heard Abel Gregg's voice from inside the stage coach. "He ain't dead . . . Sundown ain't dead!" In another moment Abel reappeared, mingled relief and concern in the look he gave the girl. "Nothing we can do until Doc Smeed gets here," he said. His eyes shifted in a sharp glance at the crossing, rested for a moment on a spiral of dust that whirled along the road beyond the river. "Looks like the doc coming now," he added. "I reckon Pablo must have scared him plenty — the way he's got them black Morgans on the dead run."

There was a brief silence as the three watched the high-topped buggy careening along behind the galloping team. Abel said in his placid voice, "He'll have to slow down for the crossin' if he don't want a bad spill." He shook his head. "Doc always drives like a wild Injun."

The younger man sensed that he was giving the girl time to get hold of herself. Abel went on in the same easy conversational tone. "You handled them doggone mules awful smart, Benita. You couldn't stop 'em, but you kept 'em on the road." His smile went to the tall stranger. "Would have been a bad spill, though, if this

6

young feller hadn't headed you before you hit the crossin'."

The girl nodded, drew in a long breath. She was less pale, and a faint smile broke the tautness of her face. "I've never been so frightened," she admitted with a repressed shudder. "Abel is right. I can't thank you enough for — for what you did —" She broke off, her look questioning Abel.

"Never laid eyes on him before," Abel said with a grin. "Didn't stop to ask him his name."

"Rand Kenzie," drawled the young man. A smile glinted in his blue eyes. "The thanks go to Abel at that. He was the one to size up the situation."

"I'm Benita Ellison," the girl said. "You can't tell me anything about Abel Gregg. He's my best friend. And you can't pretend you haven't just saved my life," she added soberly.

"Rand Kenzie, huh?" Abel's voice was softly musing, his eyes shrewdly bright. "Seems to me I've heard that name before some place."

"I'm a stranger in the Palo Pinto country," Rand Kenzie said. A subtle inflection of voice, the flicker in his eyes conveyed a warning that decided Abel to change the subject.

"Looks like Pablo has spread the news plenty," he said, shifting his gaze to the approaching buggy now splashing across the shallows of the Palo Pinto. Some half score riders were lifting dust on the road beyond.

There was another silence, broken by Benita Ellison's low voice. "It happened up in Piñon Pass," she said.

"Any notion who done the shootin', Benita?" questioned Abel.

She shook her head. "There was only the one shot." She faltered. "I — I didn't know Sundown had been hit. We heard the shot — a rifle — and then Sundown screeched at the mules the way he does when he starts them into a run —"

Abel interrupted her. "Where was you settin', Benita?"

"Up on the seat with Sundown. I was the only passenger, and anyway, Sundown always has me ride up on the seat with him." She went on with her story. "I didn't know he'd been shot until he suddenly slammed hard on the brakes, and then — and then —" She faltered again. "It was terrible," she said. "Sundown seemed to be falling over the side as he jammed on the brakes with his foot. I thought he was going right down on the wheels and pulled him back across my knees." Benita paused, passed a hand before her eyes. "He was unconscious, and there was blood on him. It was terrible," she repeated with a shiver.

"You stopped the team?" Abel asked.

"We were through the pass and half way up the Red Rock grade, nearly a mile from where Sundown was shot."

Abel nodded. "Awful steep hill . . . no trouble haltin' the team on *that* climb — not with the brakes tight set."

"I couldn't bold Sundown on the seat and drive too," Benita went on. "I managed to pull him down, over the seat into the stage. It was all I could do, and I had to get away from there."

8

"Afraid they was followin' you," Abel put in with a grim nod. "You figgered right, Benita. Nothing to do but get away from there as fast as the team could run."

"That was the trouble." Benita's tone was rueful. "I kept the mules on the run, popped Sundown's whip at them for all I was worth, and then we struck the long down grade this side of the divide. It was terribly steep in places, and Abel, I couldn't reach the brake-shift with my foot. I just could not get the brakes set when we started down that awful grade."

"Sundown has mighty long legs," Abel commented. "He had those brakes set to suit his own reach." The liveryman wagged his head pityingly. "I reckon we savvy, Benita."

"The mules went mad when they found the stage rolling down on their heels," the girl said with a sharp intake of her breath.

"Clamped down on their bits and lit out, huh?" Abel's smile was grimly sympathetic. "Nothing for you to do but keep 'em in the road. Sundown couldn't have done better."

"We made some of those turns on two wheels," the girl told her listeners. Her face paled at the recollection.

"Don't let your mind hang on it too much right now," sagely counseled Abel. He added mazingly, "Mighty queer business. Don't make sense — anybody wantin' to take a potshot at Sundown Skaggs. Sundown is the milk of human kindness." Abel broke off, vaguely conscious of a curious expression in Rand Kenzie's eyes. It came and went so quickly that Abel was not at all sure he had seen correctly.

CHAPTER
TWO

Doc Smeed's black Morgans were headed across the mud flats at a fast pace, the high-topped buggy rattling at their heels. He pulled the sweating team to a halt, snatched his black bag from the seat and scrambled between the wheels.

"Who's hurt, Abel?" He flung the question bruskly, eyes under bushy, grizzled brows inquisitively scrutinizing the girl. "Hello, Benita! Don't see but what you're all right. Pablo Casado said you were killed, or going to be."

"It's old Sundown," Abel broke in with a significant gesture at the dusty stage.

"Dead?" The doctor's tone was shocked. He began to run, bag swinging in his hand.

"Looks bad," Abel said, limping in his wake. "Was afraid to touch him, Doc. I knew you'd get here quick as you could."

"Quite right." Dr. Smeed scrambled up into the stage. "Wish everybody had your good sense." He bent over the unconscious stage driver, sent a frown back at the anxious Abel. "Keep those people out," he added testily, "Don't want 'em shouting around here."

10

Abel lowered his wiry frame carefully down from the high steps and lifted a cautioning hand. "Doc says for you boys to keep quiet," he warned the newcomers.

One of the riders swung from his saddle. He was a big, powerfully made man with a harsh craggy face and coldly arrogant eyes that stabbed suspiciously at the tall stranger standing close to Benita Ellison.

"What's the trouble?" Mindful of Abel Gregg's warning he spoke in a hoarse whisper.

The girl's slim body stiffened perceptibly. "Sundown has been shot," she answered briefly.

"Damn that Mex!" The man's intolerant eyes took on a stormy look. "He was yellin' something about you being killed."

"It almost came to that," she retorted. "Thanks to Mr. Kenzie I'm still all in one piece." She smiled faintly. "And you needn't damn old Pablo, Mr. Boicer. He's my friend."

Boicer shrugged his big shoulders, fastened a hard look on the other man. "Kenzie? Your name is Kenzie?"

"I was born that way," drawled Rand. His blue eyes frosted as he met Boicer's stare. "What about it?"

Doc Smeed's voice pulled their hostile looks apart. "We've got to get him over to my place," he said to Abel Gregg. "The bullet has lodged close to his spine. I can't do a thing out here."

"He's not dead?" Boicer moved close to the stage, peered in at the unconscious man.

"He soon will be dead if we waste time here," grumbled the doctor. He looked at the girl. "Benita — you hop into my buggy and head for town. I'll want

11

Mrs. Simmons. She's helped me bring a lot of lives into the world and maybe she can help save this one from leaving it." His gaze quested around at the cluster of silently attentive riders. "One of you boys get this stage moving. Clanton — you climb inside and help me keep Sundown comfortable as we can."

"Sure," assented Boicer. "Get a lead-rope on my horse, Keno," he said to a lanky man on a bay horse.

"You can take my mare along with you, Keno," put in Abel. "*I'm* rollin' this stage in." He climbed up to the seat and gathered the lines.

Rand Kenzie followed Benita to the doctor's buggy. "Let me drive." His smile was warm on her. "You're in no shape to handle these horses." He stepped into the buggy before she could protest.

They moved off across the mud flats, the riderless buckskin following at a trot. The girl's eyes widened a bit as her glance went back at the horse.

"He's well trained," she remarked.

"Mingo has good horse sense," Rand chuckled.

They swung into the road and he let the black Morgans have their heads. The buckskin was forced to break into a gallop to keep up.

"These nags can trot," Rand commented. "They can move along."

"Dr. Smeed loves fast trotters," Benita told him. "His one dissipation, excepting poker." Her tone was affectionate.

They heard the stage rattling behind them, the pounding of hoofs. The girl's face was pale again as she glanced back. "Poor old Sundown. It is all so hateful —

mysterious. I can't imagine who would want to kill him. Everybody knows Sundown Skaggs." She was silent for a long moment, hands clasped tight in her lap. "It terrifies me," she went on in a voice he hardly heard above the rattle of the spinning wheels. "You see — my — my father was murdered last week — shot in the back." Her hands unlocked, nervously smoothed the black skirt over her knees. "I've been visiting with an aunt in Santa Fe since it happened, but I couldn't stand it away from the ranch. And there's so much to do."

He slanted a brief sidewise glance that her downcast eyes failed to note. She would have been startled at the compassion, the stark rage that flickered across his bronzed face.

"Ranch?" His tone was interested without being curious.

"Red Rock." She came out of her abstraction, eyes lifting in a quick look at him. "Red Rock Ranch, or — perhaps that doesn't mean anything to you."

"I'm a stranger here," he admitted. "Hit the town about the time Abel spotted you coming down the grade. He didn't give me time to get acquainted."

The road swooped down to the shallows of the Palo Pinto. Rand pulled the team to a walk. The girl glanced thoughtfully at the water now aglitter with sunset fires. She drew in a sharp breath, looked at her companion. "It's a good thing for me that you arrived in Palo Pinto when you did. I'd have been in the quicksands by now. The quicksands are bad on both sides of the crossing. You — you saved my life."

"I told you the thanks are due Abel," he reminded, and added soberly, "I'm going to like that old timer."

"My father thought a lot of him," Benita said simply. "This crossing is named for him," she went on. "Gregg's Crossing. He was jumped here years ago by Comanches. He was freighting supplies to Silver City."

"I've heard that story," Rand said. He was glad to switch her to things outside of herself. "That story has traveled a lot the past forty or fifty years." He chuckled. "Stood off those Comanches for three days and took a hundred scalps."

The girl laughed, shook her head. "Abel will take *your* scalp if you say that in front of him. There were not more than fifteen or twenty Indians in the war party. They killed his swampers and ran off his mules. But he *did* put up such a fight that they got tired and went off without burning his wagons or getting *his* scalp. Abel couldn't get away without mules to pull his wagons, so he unloaded some tents he had, set them up and started a town. There were a lot of gold seekers coming along, bound for the mines. Abel had tons of supplies to sell. He put up a big sign, GREGG'S CAMP and charged bonanza prices for everything he sold. Gregg's Camp was the beginning of Palo Pinto."

"I'm going to like Abel," Rand said again with an approving nod. He added dryly, "I can't say the same for Clanton Boicer."

She made no response to this, stared straight ahead; and again she missed that curious flicker of rage that ran across his face like a stab of lightning in a dark and angry sky.

14

Wind lifted and swirled their dust, and suddenly they were past Abel Gregg's big feed barn at the upper end of Palo Pinto's short wide street. A group of men and women in front of the stage office gaped at them as they flashed past. Sam Bleeker ran from his store, followed by his assistant, and across the street men spilled excitedly from the swing doors of Silver's Palace Bar.

Benita Ellison said, "The next turn to the left . . . the third house."

Rand pulled the blacks down, made the turn and in another moment the buggy was at a standstill in front of a neat whitewashed cabin behind a whitewashed picket fence. Benita scrambled out between the wheels, pushed through the gate which was flanked by two huge chinaberry trees. A woman appeared in the doorway. She uttered a cry of mingled surprise and pleasure.

"Benita, darlin'! You're a sight for sore eyes. I'm that glad to see you . . . and when did you get back from Santa Fe?" Her arms went around the girl in a warm hug. And then, alarm in her voice, "For why do you look so upset, lass? What is wrong?"

"Dr. Smeed wants you at his office," Benita said. There was a choke in her voice. "Sundown Skaggs has been shot."

"You don't say!" ejaculated Mrs. Simmons. She was a comely, middle-aged woman with a touch of gray in her black hair and shrewd, kindly eyes in a weather-beaten face. "I'll hurry over, lass." She was already making a right-about-face for her door.

"We'll wait for you, Nora," called the girl. She returned to the buggy. Her troubled look went past Rand to the fast-moving dust beyond the town. Abel was making good time with the stage.

Rand read her thoughts, said comfortingly, "Dr. Smeed is with him. I wouldn't worry too much, Miss Ellison."

"It's so hateful —" She spoke fiercely. "My father — and now poor old Sundown. I — I don't understand!"

The cabin door slammed shut and Mrs. Simmons ran down the flower-bordered walk. The gate flew open before her charge and she paused at the girl's side, a bit breathless, but businesslike. "It's a tight squeeze —" She scrambled into the buggy and pulled the girl into her lap. "All right, young feller — let's go."

"Mr. Kenzie," Benita introduced as Rand swung the team in a sharp turn back to the main street. "He saved my life," she added.

"You don't say!" Excitement deepened the Irish lilt in Mrs. Simmons' voice. "There's plenty been happenin', it seems to me."

"Plenty," Benita said. Rand felt the shiver of her slim body. She spoke again, directing him, and in less than five minutes they were halted in front of the doctor's house which stood on the brink of an arroyo some hundred yards beyond the hotel.

Mrs. Simmons sprang down. Benita followed her, spoke briefly to an old Indian who appeared from back of the house.

"Me take," the Indian said to Rand. He climbed into the buggy and Rand went to the buckskin horse, stood watching the approaching stage. A score or more horsemen, and men running on foot, trailed behind in the dust.

The first out of the stage was Clanton Boicer. He made for the girl standing by Mrs. Simmons, but his look went angrily to Rand who was tying the buckskin to the hitchrail under a cottonwood tree. "That jasper had a nerve," Boicer said. "I saw him climb into the buggy."

"Mr. Kenzie was very kind." Benita turned abruptly and followed Mrs. Simmons into the house. A quick glance from the door told her that gentle hands were lifting the wounded stage driver down from the coach.

Boicer heard a low-spoken voice at his shoulder. "Who shot him, Clant? Was it a holdup?"

The big man's face turned, met Sam Bleeker's inquisitive eyes. His own eyes went cold, wary. "We're all asking the same question, Sam."

Sam Bleeker asked in the same low, cautious voice, "Who's the feller the Ellison girl had with her in the doc's buggy?" He flicked a look across at Rand Kenzie.

"You might ask him," growled Boicer. "I don't know all the bums that hit this town." He pushed through the crowd goggling at the gate and disappeared inside the house.

Abel Gregg had climbed from the stage and was talking to a stubby, bow-legged man with a shock of straw-colored hair under a battered sombrero. "No baggage, 'cept Miss Ellison's trunk, Shorty. I reckon she'll be stoppin' at the hotel tonight."

Shorty climbed up to the driver's seat and gathered the lines into freckled hands. "I'll drop the trunk over to the hotel," he said. His look shifted to Sam Bleeker. "Hop up, Sam. You'll be wantin' the mail pouch. I'll stop in at the store first."

"Sure," agreed Sam. He was the postmaster. "Looks like some feller tried to pull a holdup," he said to Abel. He repeated the question he had put to Clanton Boicer. "Who's the feller come in with Benita Ellison in the doc's buggy?"

"Him?" Abel's eyes idled across at Rand Kenzie still motionless by the side of his horse. "He told me his name is Kenzie — if that means anything to you, Sam."

The storekeeper shook his head. "Never heard of him before. Was wondering how come he was in the doc's buggy with Benita." He scrambled up to the seat. "All right, Shorty . . . let's get the mail unloaded. She's late enough."

Abel stood watching while Shorty Tod swung the mules into the turn, then he went slowly to Rand who gave him a keen look. "The doc says he's got a chance, son." Abel paused, fumbled in a pocket and stared at the plug of tobacco in his fingers. He seemed uneasy. "Staying in town?" His eyes lifted in a sharp look.

"I don't know for how long." Rand's gaze was on the doctor's door. "I was planning to put up my buck horse at your barn. I reckon that hotel keeps rooms for passing strangers." His drawling voice took on an edge. "Any reason why I shouldn't stay in this cowtown?"

Abel slowly returned the plug of tobacco to his pocket. Worry deepened the creases in his face. "That's a question for *you* to answer, Kenzie." His voice was low, beyond the hearing of the restless crowd surging at the doctor's gate. "I just want you to know that Clant Boicer don't think any too well of you."

"Who is Clant Boicer?" Rand shook his head. "I know who you mean — but who is he?"

"Clant is sheriff of Palo Pinto County . . . owns the Rafter B that borders Ben Ellison's Red Rock Ranch."

Rand Kenzie's long hard body stiffened, a bootheel stirred, sent out a rasp of dragging spur, his eyes went frosty. Abel was watching him. He went on in the same low, cautious voice, "Clant done some talkin' there in the stage as we come along. He figgers you are the feller that filled Ben Ellison's back with buckshot."

"Do you think the same way, Abel?" The young man's voice was cool, almost amused.

The old frontiersman reached angrily for his tobacco, bit off a chew. "Don't be a doggone fool. I know a man when I see him."

"Meaning what?" drawled Rand. His blue eyes held a warm look.

"I mean that Clant Boicer is loco." Abel spat out a dark brown stream, chewed vigorously on the bulging plug. "He's got ideas about you, son."

The doctor's screen door slammed open, framed Boicer's big-shouldered body. Abel Gregg spoke in a low whisper, his eyes hard on the man in the doorway. "I mean that Clant figgers to throw you in jail for the murder of Ben Ellison." His voice took on a pleading note. "Fork that buck horse, Kenzie. Get movin' — *before it's too late.*"

19

CHAPTER
THREE

There was no doubting the purpose in Clant Boicer's mind. Rand knew that Abel was telling him the truth, and that it was either immediate flight, or seeing the inside of Palo Pinto's jail. Nevertheless, he shook his head, said briefly, "I'm not running away, Abel."

"Clant's the sheriff." Abel's tone was urgent. "You can't buck the law. Make things worse for you if you go resisting him."

"Boicer is a fool — if he thinks he can pin a murder on me," Rand said contemptuously. "Let him put me in his jail. He can't keep me there for long."

The sheriff paused outside the gate, spoke briefly to several men in the crowd. Rand was conscious of quick, hard looks from them. He spoke quietly to the liveryman. "Take care of my buck horse for me, Abel."

"I'll do that," Abel promised simply. "Anything else, son?"

Rand hesitated, gaze on the approaching men. "I'd like you to tell Miss Ellison your idea of it," he said. "I'd hate her to think what Boicer thinks, or pretends to think."

"You bet I'll tell her." Abel spoke gruffly. "Benita will take my word against Clant Boicer any day in the week."

"She told me you were her best friend," smiled Rand.

"There's nothin' I won't do for Ben Ellison's daughter," declared the old man. "You bet I'm her friend. She's needin' friends right now," he added with a grim shake of his head.

Boicer and the three men with him were pushing purposefully through the crowd in front of the gate. Rand said quickly, "Abel, keep this gun for me." He drew the Colt from his holster with a swift motion and handed it to the other man. Abel stuck the .45 inside his belt.

"I'll keep her safe for you, son," he promised.

"I'm trusting you a lot," Rand told him a bit grimly. "If things get bad, Abel, there's something hidden under the silver butt-plate that can help me. I'm leaving it to you."

"I savvy," Abel grunted.

"I don't want it used if I can work out of this in any other way," Rand said in a low, hurried voice. Boicer and his three companions were moving toward them with quick steps, hands on holstered guns.

"You can trust me," Abel assured him.

Boicer's voice broke in, harsh, arrogant. "Put up your hands, Kenzie." His gun was out. "You're under arrest."

"Arrest?" Rand's tone was mildly surprised, held a hint of amusement. "What's the joke, Boicer?"

"No joke," retorted the sheriff. "Put up your hands. We're not taking chances with a killer."

Rand looked coolly at the four men confronting him, their guns menacing. "I'm not wearing a gun, Boicer," he said. He lifted his hands. "Anything to oblige." He chuckled.

"Look him over, Ketcher," the sheriff said to one of the deputies.

"Nothin' on him," Ketcher announced, after a brief but thorough search.

Boicer looked suspiciously at the Colt stuck inside Abel's belt. He knew the liveryman was not in the habit of wearing a gun. Whatever his thoughts about it he kept them to himself. Abel Gregg was not one for even the sheriff of Palo Pinto to challenge.

"All right, boys," he said gruffly. "Get him over to the jail."

"Just a moment," objected Rand. "I'm a stranger in this town. Just got in, and here you go, throwing me into your jail. What's the idea, Boicer? Trying to make out I shot old Sundown Skaggs?" His tone was ironical.

Boicer said heavily, "I'm arresting you for the murder of Ben Ellison."

"You're crazy," retorted Rand. "I've never seen Ben Ellison in my life."

Sheriff Boicer favored him with a thin smile. "We don't expect you to admit it." His tone was derisive. "Killers don't admit nothin'."

"What's the proof?" Rand wanted to know with some heat. "You have no proof," he added. "This is a frame-up, Boicer."

"We've plenty proof," rejoined the sheriff. His look went briefly to the black-maned buckskin. "The killer of Ben Ellison was riding that horse."

"A lie," Rand declared. "The killer might have been riding a buckskin, but not my Mingo."

"I know the horses in this county," Boicer said with a shrug. "Plenty of buckskins, black manes and tails." A hint of grudging admiration crept into his eyes as he studied Mingo. "You can take it from me there's no other horse in these parts just like this buckskin of yours. He ain't a true buckskin. His hide is more creamy gold than buckskin."

"That's right," agreed Ketcher. "If his mane and tail was silver 'stead of jet black, he'd be a Palomino." A covetous gleam was in the man's unpleasant eyes. "A damn good bronc, whatever he is," he added.

"You can go to the top of the class," grinned Rand. "His daddy and his mama were both silver-maned Palominos. Mingo's a sport — and he's all horse." His look went meaningly to Abel Gregg. "I'm trusting you to look after him for me, Abel. He's stall broke and gentle as a kitten."

"You bet Abel will look after him," the sheriff broke in gruffly. "That horse is going to be evidence in a murder trial." He gave the liveryman a hard look. "I'm holding you responsible for that horse."

"I'll keep him safe," Abel rejoined with some tartness. He gave Rand a reassuring grin. "That's a promise," he added, more for the prisoner's benefit than the sheriff's.

Benita Ellison appeared in the doctor's doorway as the deputies led Rand away, followed by Boicer. Amazement widened her dark eyes. The meaning of that little group of men walking up the street was only too plain. Her hand went up in a futile gesture of protest, then she was running down the walk and through the gate. Curious eyes followed her as she overtook Abel and the buckskin horse. The liveryman gave her a troubled look.

"What — what is it?" She asked the question breathlessly, gestured at the little group of men disappearing around the corner into the main street. "What — what are they doing to Mr. Kenzie?"

"You won't like it, Benita." Abel spoke in a distressed voice. "Clant Boicer's got a fool notion that young Kenzie is a killer."

"You mean he's arrested?"

"That's about it," Abel admitted. He caressed the buckskin's velvety nose with a horny palm. "Kenzie asked me to look after his horse for him."

Benita was looking at him with dilated eyes. "I don't believe it." She spoke fiercely. "Nothing can make me believe he's a — a killer." Something she read in the old man's face stiffened her attention on him. Her smooth cheeks went white. "You mean that Clant thinks he's the man who murdered father?" She was horrified.

"That's about it," repeated Abel. He would have given anything to have spared her the shock. Rand Kenzie had just saved her life, and now he was being walked off to the jail, charged with the murder of her father. He added pityingly, "Don't take it too hard,

24

Benita. I know men, and I know young Kenzie ain't the kind to fill a man's back with buckshot. He's a fighter, but he ain't a sneakin' murderer. Clant Boicer has pulled off a fool play and he'll sure eat plenty dirt before he's done with it."

Benita looked at him in silence, her eyes bright with unshed tears. Abel touched her arm gently. "We'll get him out of that jail in no time at all," he reassured her.

"I can't bear it!" she said miserably. "I — I hate Clanton Boicer. He — he's doing this to — to spite me."

Abel nodded. "Clant was some peeved, you lettin' Kenzie drive you back to town in the buggy," he admitted. "Did some cussin' back inside the stage."

She showed a certain relief for some reason, but her anger mounted. "It's a mean trick to punish Mr. Kenzie," she declared. She paused, added thoughtfully. "Abel — I must see Mr. Kenzie. I want him to know how I feel about it." Her voice faltered. "I can't bear it — for him to think that perhaps *I* think the way Clanton Boicer does."

"You'll be at the hotel for the night?" Abel looked at her questioningly.

"Yes. Nobody at the ranch was expecting me back so soon. I was planning to have you drive me over tomorrow."

"I told Shorty Tod to drop your trunk at the hotel," Abel said. He hesitated, glanced back at the doctor's house. "How's it goin' with Sundown?"

Benita's thoughts were far away from old Sundown Skaggs at that moment. She came to with a start.

"Sundown? Why — Dr. Smeed thinks he will be all right." She smiled faintly. "He's, able to talk, at least I heard him swearing."

"Sundown can cuss proper when he's wound up," Abel said. His eyes narrowed in a speculative look down the street. The man riding out of the arroyo was Tony Silver. A bulging canvas bag hung from saddle-horn. Abel gave the girl a slow smile. "Looks like Tony has bagged him a mess of quail," he said. "There's plenty quail down in the arroyo this year." He chuckled. "You'll be eatin' quail tonight if you've a mind to."

They followed the excitedly speculating crowd that straggled in the wake of the sheriff and his prisoner. "I'll see you soon," Benita said when they came abreast of the dingy little hotel.

She sent a brief look at the men clattering along the board sidewalk, bit her lip and went quickly inside. Rand's head turned in time for him to glimpse the flutter of her trim black skirt as she disappeared. His face went a deep red. She would have heard the news by now.

A man standing in the doorway of a small frame building next to the ornately fronted Silver Palace Bar, spoke to the sheriff. "What's up, Clant? Hooked a prisoner?"

Boicer halted, a malicious grin on his face. "You won't have a chance to fix up bail money for *this* jasper, Lark."

"Murder charge?" Rand felt the play of the man's keen eyes. Almost mechanically his own eyes took in the neat gold letters on the office window.

26

LARKIN ISWELL
ATTORNEY AT LAW
LOANS

"You won't want to touch the case, Lark," gloated Sheriff Boicer. "Not when you know he's the feller that killed Ben Ellison." It was obvious that he disliked the lawyer. "This man is goin' to swing."

Larkin Iswell's face showed no hint of his thoughts. He was a small, thin man with features that ran to sharpness under a bulging forehead. His eyes were bright and ferrety, his long nose and chin pointed and his thin-lipped mouth had the tight set of a steel trap. He had mouse-colored hair, neatly parted in the middle. A fastidious dresser, from the looks of his carefully pressed linen suit and big diamond pin in black tie.

He said in a hard, metallic voice, "Good work, Clant. Nobody in this town will be more pleased than I to see the killer of Ben Ellison swing."

Rand was again conscious of that brief scrutinizing look from the man's ferrety eyes. He moved on with the deputies, heard Iswell say, "I'll want a talk with him, Clant." The sheriff's voice, low, angry, reached him as the deputies hustled him around the corner. "What the hell for should *you* want to talk to the jasper. I won't stand for your tricks, Lark." He heard no more, only the clatter of the sheriff's bootheels as Boicer hurried to overtake them.

The jail office was a small, untidy room furnished with a cheap pine table and several wooden chairs.

Rifles, and a sawed-off shotgun stood in one corner and an array of short guns hung from pegs behind the littered desk. What immediately caught Rand's eyes was a brand new reward notice conspicuous among the fly-specked advertisements of men wanted by the law.

$1000.00 REWARD WILL BE
PAID FOR THE ARREST DEAD
OR ALIVE OF THE MAN WHO
KILLED BENJAMIN ELLISON

Sheriff Boicer saw his look, grinned at him. "That's what *this* town thinks about it," he said. He winked at his deputies. "You'll be lucky if you stay in this jail long enough to stand trial."

"That's the shoutin' truth," grinned Ketcher.

A bulky fat man suddenly loomed in the corridor doorway. He had a large pink face covered with a stubble of sandy beard and his bloodshot, bulging eyes took on a resentful look as he stared at the prisoner. "I ain't goin' to be held responsible for the skunk if he's the killer of Ben Ellison," he grumbled. Tobacco juice dribbled from the corner of pendulous lower lip.

"You'll do your duty as jailer, and no more," reassured the sheriff with another grin at Rand. "I ain't asking you to fight off no mobs, Fat."

"I don't aim to," declared the jailer. He shambled back into the corridor. "All right, fellers. Let's lock him up."

The cell door shut with an ominous clang and for a long moment the sheriff stared in silence at the man behind the bars. It was plain that he was enjoying his triumph, and when he spoke the source of his feeling was equally obvious to the prisoner. "Benita Ellison is goin' to be mighty peeved when she learns she was riding so chummy with the man who murdered her own dad," he said with relish.

"So that's it?" Rand retorted with a thin smile.

"That — and a lot more." Boicer's grin was malevolent. "You ain't fooled me none, *Mister* Kenzie, which ain't your name I'll bet my star."

Rand looked at him in stony silence. The sheriff indulged in a low, amused laugh and turned on his heel. The two deputies and the fat jailer followed him down the dark corridor. Rand heard the slam of the door.

CHAPTER
FOUR

He stood for a long minute, rigid, his expression strained, decidedly worried. A slow smile suddenly relaxed the taut lines on his face. He fumbled in his shirt pocket, drew out empty fingers with an annoyed shake of his head. His tobacco and papers had been removed, along with other belongings.

His look went appraisingly around the cell. The Palo Pinto jail offered little in the way of comfort for its guests. A pile of dirty straw in one corner, and nothing else. A small window, secured with an iron grating, stood shoulder high in the outer adobe wall. He moved across to it, pulled tentatively at the iron bars, turned away with a hopeless shrug and went back to the cell door. He pressed close to the bars, listened intently. Voices came to him faintly from the office. The squeaky, protesting voice of the fat jailer, a lower, thin, hard voice; and suddenly the office door opened and Rand saw two men approaching down the corridor.

He was not surprised to recognize the sharp-featured little lawyer. There had been a message in that last look Iswell had darted at him.

"I ain't unlocking the cell," grumbled the jailer. "You can do your talkin' through the bars. At that I ain't doin' right. Clant said for me to let nobody get to see him."

"This man has a right to a lawyer," snapped Iswell.

"I know the law, Fat, if you and the sheriff don't. Get out," he added. "I'm talking to him alone."

Fat went off, muttering to himself. Iswell sent an urbane smile through the bars at the interested prisoner. "You're in a tight spot — a very tight spot." He spoke softly.

"Not the first time." Rand was watching him.

"I don't think you killed Ben Ellison," the lawyer said surprisingly.

"Well — as a matter of fact, I didn't." Rand smiled. "Too bad you can't make the sheriff think the same."

"Boicer is a stubborn fool." Iswell's tone was a sneer. "He claims your name is not Kenzie . . . claims you're Ringer Barran."

"I've heard of Ringer Barran," Rand said cautiously. A guard seemed to lower over his eyes.

"Who hasn't?" A gargoyle smile spread over the lawyer's face. "Barran has more sheriffs yappin' on his tail than any killer outlaw in the southwest."

"I've heard talk about him," admitted Rand in the same cautious tone. "He's a hired killer . . . asks big money for a job."

"You look a lot like him," Iswell said significantly. "He's a good-looker, for all he's a deadly snake."

"Thanks for the compliment." Rand's smile was grim. He added ironically, "What are you driving at. Offering your legal services?" He shook his head. "Bail money is no good on a murder charge."

"No good at all," agreed the lawyer. "And I'm not going to court for you, Kenzie, or Barran, if you really *are* Barran."

"I'm not Barran."

"We'll let it pass," Iswell said with an airy gesture. "It's just my notion you didn't kill Ben Elision." Again his gargoyle smile. "I'm soft-hearted . . . don't like to see an innocent man swing, or go to the pen."

"Get to the point," urged Rand.

"We've got to get you out of this jail, and damn soon," Iswell told him briskly. "The murderer of Ben Ellison will never stand trail . . . not in this town."

"I savvy," Rand said laconically.

"Boicer won't do much trying to break up a mob," Iswell told him with heavy emphasis.

"Getting out of this jail doesn't look so easy," pointed out Rand dryly.

"We've got to break you out," asserted the lawyer.

"Won't you be risking a lot?" Rand asked. His thoughts were racing behind the mask of his face.

Iswell smiled. "I told you I'm some soft-hearted," he reminded. "A bit of a Don Quixote if you like."

"Just how will you break me out of here?" Rand forced a note of excitement, rising hope, into his voice.

"Leave it to me," reassured the lawyer with another airy gesture. "I'll arrange things . . . have a horse ready for your getaway."

Rand's eyes measured the grating at the window. "Through there?" He asked the question thoughtfully.

Iswell nodded. "The moon will be down early. Be ready to catch the rope and make it double fast to the

32

bars. There'll be three ropes," he added. "And three men on horses outside. They'll snake that grating out easy as swallowing a piece of pie. Nothing for you to do but squeeze through, get to the horse and head for the border."

"Sounds good to me," Rand said with a show of increasing excitement. "I'll sure be all set to go." He grinned.

The lawyer produced a cigar from a vest pocket, carefully punctured the end with a gold toothpick that dangled from his watch-chain. "It's a risk," he warned gravely, "a big risk — but it's that — or your neck." He lighted the cigar, blew out a mouthful of smoke, eyes intent on the prisoner's face.

"I'm used to risks," Rand said laconically. "Those buzzards took my tobacco," he added wistfully.

Iswell's fingers reached into his vest pocket. "Fat Wiler won't like it, but I'll take *this* risk." He chuckled, thrust the cigar between the bars.

"I never was much of a cigar smoker," Rand said. "Any port in a storm, and I sure crave the feel of tobacco smoke."

Iswell struck a match, held the light to the cigar. "You needn't admit I gave it to you." He smiled.

"I won't," promised Rand with a grin. He drew luxuriously on the cigar.

Iswell turned on his heel, looked back, eyes very bright. "When the moon's down," he reminded softly. "Be ready, Barran."

"Kenzie," Rand said, "the name is Kenzie."

"Anything you like," smiled the lawyer. "Just remember one thing, I'm a man who stands for fair play. That is why I'm helping you in the only way possible." He vanished down the dark corridor. Rand heard the door open, slam shut on its heavy spring.

He moved swiftly to the small window, again tested the iron grating with strongly pulling fingers. Three men on horses, with tough ropes could do the job, but not the bare hands of a lone man.

His mind was racing, functioning with the easy precision of a well-oiled machine. Larkin Iswell's astonishing offer to break him out of jail was too good to be true. The thing was fishy. Rand was puzzled, conscious of growing apprehensions. He wished old Abel Gregg would put in an appearance. He felt the urgent need of a great haste. The early moonlight was already filtering in through the grating. Another three hours and the moon would be down, and horsemen would be outside the window, with ropes to snatch the grating from the adobe wall. Outside a horse was to be waiting for him — and a fast run for the border.

Rand drew hard on the cigar, let out a mouthful of the fragrant smoke. Iswell smoked good cigars. The man was fastidious, obviously a lover of the good things in life. His immaculate, well-pressed linen suit, the big diamond in his tie, the well-kept finger-nails of his delicate, clawlike hands. And yet there was something repulsive about him, a reptilian look.

The door down the corridor opened. Rand heard the jailer's shambling feet. He hurriedly tucked the cigar between the bars of the window grating, lighted end toward the dark night, then he moved back to the cell door.

The jailer was carrying a lantern in one hand. He came close to the cell door, peered at the prisoner, sniffed suspiciously. "Lark sure smoked plenty when he was in here," he grumbled. There was a pronounced thickness in his voice. "At that he ain't a bad scout. Give me a full flask of whiskey, which ain't like him at all. Lark Iswell ain't what you call a free-handed gent."

The jailer suddenly lifted the lantern, peered closely through the bars, suspicion welling from his large pink face. Apparently satisfied nothing was amiss with his prisoner, he lowered the lantern to the floor and produced a flask from his hip pocket. "He told me things about you," he said in a curiously awed voice. "I'm sure peeved at Clant for not puttin' me wise."

"About what?" Rand asked softly from the dark cell.

The jailer put the flask to his lips, gurgled noisily. He returned the flask to his pocket, stared with a hint of admiration in his bloodshot eyes. "Lark was tellin' me you're Ringer Barran." Satisfaction oozed in his words. "I reckon my jail is the first jail ever held that damn outlaw."

"Didn't your sheriff tell you?" queried Rand.

"Clant sure forgot his manners to me," grumbled the jailer. "I reckon he was too excited, or somethin'." He chuckled. "Clant's kind of new at the sheriff bus'ness." His bulbous nose wrinkled in a suspicious sniff. "That cigar smoke sure hangs awful thick in here."

"How about something to eat," Rand asked. Food was far from his thoughts at that moment. He wanted to get the jailer's mind away from the cigar smoke.

"Nothin' doin' till mornin'," announced Fat. The glimmer of lantern light showed a malicious leer on his face. He reached for his flask, took another long gurgling drink. "I'll sure get my name in the Santa Fe papers . . . holdin' Ringer Barran in my jail," he added as he put the bottle away.

A banging in the office drew his head around and muttering an oath he shambled down the corridor with the lantern.

Rand listened, ears sharpened with renewed hope. Abel Gregg!

He heard the muffled sound of arguing voices. The door opened, lantern light danced along the corridor, threw grotesque shadows of two men approaching the cell. Rand let out a sigh of relief as he recognized Abel Gregg's quiet voice.

Caution warned him to show no signs of pleasure. He stood motionless, his face a mask as the jailer lifted the lantern into a full glare on him. "Here's a feller wants to talk to you." His tone was sulky.

"That's right." Abel spoke placidly. "You don't need to wait, Fat."

"Fust come Lark Iswell, and now it's you," complained the jailer. He hiccoughed. "I reckon this a-here Ringer Barran is sure important, and if you wasn't Abel Gregg I sure would tell you to get to hell out of here."

"You've been drinking," Abel said severely. "Leave me alone with this man, Fat."

"I sure got a right to take a drink," defended the jailer. "Don't hold Ringer Barran in my jail every day." He guffawed, reached unblushingly for his flask. "All right, Abel. I'm giving you five minutes with this killer hombre." His shambling tread died away down the corridor. The door slammed.

Abel lifted the lantern from the floor, turned its glow on the prisoner. "How's it coming, son?" His tone was quizzical, mixed with anxiety.

"I'm Ringer Barran, and a man named Iswell has been in with a promise to break me out of jail when the moon is down." Amusement lurked in Rand's voice.

"Lark Iswell!" Abel's voice sharpened. "He was in here?"

"He was — and he's got it all fixed for a jail-break." Rand swung on his heel, went swiftly to the window and recovered the cigar. He went back to the cell door, puffing hard on the lingering spark of life. "Iswell gave me this cigar," he chuckled.

"No savvy," grunted Abel.

"I do." Rand puffed out a cloud of fragrant smoke. "Your lawyer friend is fixing a booby trap."

"Lark Iswell ain't no friend of mine." Abel's eyes took on the look of cold sheet metal under the lantern's gleam. "Benita Ellison wants to see you," he added. "She's awful worried."

The cigar's red glow faded. Rand removed it, stopped, put it under his bootheel. "Worried?" His voice was hardly a whisper.

"Benita don't believe Clant Boicer's talk," Abel said in his quiet voice. "She just don't believe it, Rand."

"Abel!" There was a new brightness in the prisoner's voice. "You've told me something I wanted to know."

"You can believe it, son."

"From you, I do." There was a brief silence, and the two men stared at each other in the faint glow of the lantern's light. "I've got to get out of here," Rand said. His bootheel ground hard on the smoldering cigar butt. "Before the moon is down, Abel."

"I'm stumped," Abel admitted frankly.

"Listen!" Rand spoke in a low, tense whisper, eyes on the door down the corridor. "This thing is awfully complicated, Abel . . . and no time for talk."

"I'm listening." The old mountain man's tone was grim. "You say Lark Iswell's fixin' to break you out of this jail. He's a snake, Rand, which is why I'm listening."

Rand gave him a brief account of the lawyer's visit, the thinly veiled threat of a lynching at the hands of the murdered Ben Ellison's friends.

"Don't seem natcheral," agreed Abel. "I sure no savvy why Lark Iswell would want to help the man Clant Boicer claims is the killer of Ben Ellison."

Rand gave him a questioning look. "I'm guessing that Boicer and Iswell are not too fond of each other. Or am I on the wrong track?"

"You read sign good, son." Abel paused, his keen eyes thoughtful. "You figger Iswell is up to some trick — with his talk about breaking you loose from this jail?"

"Smells bad," drawled Rand. "You know Iswell . . . he's your fellow-townsman. I've known him less than ten minutes."

"Lark Iswell has been in Palo Pinto some five years," Abel said dryly. "I'm thinkin' it's some five years too long."

"You've answered your own question." Rand spoke in a hard voice. "That's why I've got to get out of this place inside the next hour."

"Meanin' you don't trust Lark Iswell?" The old liveryman's look went back to the door down the corridor. "Talk fast, son. Looks like Fat has got his ear cocked this way. He's half soused, but I'm telling you he's one mean hombre."

Rand pressed close against the cell bars. "Abel . . . my gun —"

"Locked safe in my desk," reassured the old man.

"Open up that silver plate on the butt," Rand told him tersely. "You'll find a piece of paper. You'll know what to do when you read it."

Abel nodded. "Sure. I savvy."

The feeble lantern light framed Rand's face against the blackness of the cell, a grim, hard face. He said quietly, "Fix it to keep Miss Ellison in her room at the hotel."

"I'll do that, too," assented Abel. He added in his placid voice, "I'm putting plenty trust in you, son."

"I'm thinking the same thing." Rand's smile reached out to him through the bars, warm, grateful. "I didn't need Benita Ellison to tell me that you're a man to tie to, Abel."

"She said that about me, huh?" A smile crinkled the old man's eyes. "I'd go to hell and back for that girl of Ben Ellison's, son."

Rand's hands fastened tight on the bars, and he said simply, "I'm in this town on her account, Abel. Keep it under your hat, and for the love of Pete, get busy with that gun of mine."

Abel hesitated, his face worried. "You're goin' ahead with this jail-break stunt of Iswell's?"

"I'm not." Rand's tone was enigmatic. "Only one more thing I want you to do — right now."

"I ain't got a gun on me," Abel told him. "I'd sure pass it to you. I could maybe grab one of them short guns Fat has hangin' on the wall in the office."

Rand shook his head. "He'll be watching you, and a misplay won't help things. Just tell Fat I'm taken awful sick."

"Don't make sense," demurred Abel. He picked up the lantern, turned away reluctantly.

Rand stood watching at the cell door until the flickering shadows suddenly were lost behind the door at the far end of the corridor. He glanced behind him at the window. Moonlight slanted down between the bars of the grating, laced the straw with silver.

CHAPTER
FIVE

The moments passed, seemed like hours, and suddenly the door down the corridor swung open. Rand drew back from the cell door, watched the dancing shadow on the wall. There was a pronounced drag to the jailer's shambling feet. Rand moved quickly back to the pile of straw, flung himself face down, arms outstretched. Moonlight played across him, showed his long body heaving convulsively.

The jailer muttered an oath as he stared through the bars. "Sick, huh? Abel said he was awful bad . . . figgered he'd took poison." He placed the lantern on the floor and reached for the keys in his pocket. "Ain't goin' to let the skunk pass out on me . . . not in *this* jail." He fumbled with the keys on the ring, made a selection. "Ringer Barran ain't goin' to die in a cell on *my* hands. First jail that damn outlaw's ever seen the insides of and I sure aim to keep him alive for the sheriff to swing proper." Swaying unsteadily Fat inserted the key and unlocked the door. He stood for a long moment, peering drunkenly at the recumbent man on the pile of straw.

"What the hell's wrong with you, feller?" Fat's tone was fretful, aggrieved. Fear widened his mean little eyes as the shudders suddenly ceased. "Hell — he's gone an' died on me." He went reeling across the floor, bent over the inert form of the prisoner, uttered a strangled oath as Rand turned with the speed of lightning and fastened his hands around his throat.

There were hard muscles under the jailer's layers of fat. He fought desperately, wrenched free from Rand's grasp and wrapped fingers over the butt of the gun in his belt. Rand drove an elbow into the man's eye. The jailer groaned and the next instant Rand had the gun in his hand. There was no mercy in him. It was not a time for generous instincts. The jailer and his friends would have small mercy for him if this attempt failed. He struck hard, felt the bulky body under him go limp.

The glow from the lantern on the corridor floor dimly lighted the scene. Rand stood up, stared intently at the gash laid open on the man's head by the gun barrel. Blood oozed from the wound, but the damage was not serious. Fat would be dead to the world for several minutes.

A hasty search of the man's pockets delivered a bunch of keys and a pair of handcuffs. Rand dropped the keys into his own pocket, removed the cartridge-laden gun-belt and buckled it around his own lean waist. He saw Fat's handkerchief trailing from a hip-pocket, snatched it and secured a gag over the jailer's mouth and finished the job by handcuffing his hands behind his back.

Satisfied, he went quickly out to the corridor, shut the cell door and turned the key that was in the lock. Pocketing the key, he picked up the lantern and went on swift, soundless feet down the corridor. A cautious look told him that the office was empty. He stepped inside, locked the corridor door. A lamp stood on the desk. He lowered the wick and blew out the light, and lantern in hand turned and looked at the array of rifles and short guns on the wall. He saw his own confiscated gun-belt, shed the one he had taken from the jailer and buckled it on, then working swiftly but carefully, he emptied the cartridges from the rifles and six-guns into a small gunny bag, along with several filled boxes of ammunition he found in a desk drawer.

He left the lantern on the desk and peered warily into the moonlit night. The jail stood on a low hill back of the town. To the right, beyond a straggly growth of junipers was Abel Gregg's livery barn, to the left he could make out the faint glow of the big kerosene lamps in front of the hotel and the saloon.

Apparently the way was clear for a stealthy dash through the junipers to the livery barn. Rand picked up the bag of confiscated cartridges and started through the door. With a shock of dismay he suddenly saw a vague shape turn up the slope from the left. He stepped back, gently pulled the door shut and drew Fat's .45 from holster.

The crunch of bootheels came up swiftly. Rand eased back to one side of the door. There was confidence and authority in that approaching tread and a quick thrill of elation ran through him. The sheriff was due for a surprise.

The door pushed open and Boicer stepped inside. He came to a shocked standstill, slowly lifted his hands in response to the low whispered command, the hard press of the gun that Rand stuck against his spine.

"Keep 'em up," Rand warned.

Boicer's head craned in a horrified look at the man he had thought was safely locked away in a cell.

"What the —" he began.

"Save your breath," crisply ordered Rand. "I'm in a hurry." He snatched a pair of handcuffs from the desk. "Stick your hands behind your back." A prod of the gun emphasized the command.

Boicer obeyed. His face was gray in the faint glow of the lantern. Rand snapped the cuffs over the sheriff's wrists.

"I'm giving you a taste of your own jail," he said with an amused chuckle. He unlocked the corridor door. "All right, sheriff, which is your favorite cell — the one you keep for really tough jaspers?"

Boicer cursed him in low bitter words. Rand prodded him hard with the gun. "Your own fault for picking on me," he said. He fished a key from his pocket and unlocked the cell that held the still unconscious jailer and motioned for the sheriff to enter. "Down on your belly," he ordered.

The sheriff gave Fat a startled look, silently stretched face down on the mud floor. Rand bent over him, gun pressed against Boicer's head. "I'm asking you a question before I tie your mouth up," he said softly. "Did you tell Iswell that I'm Ringer Barran, or did Iswell tell you?"

Boicer shifted his head for a look at the man bending over him. The amazement in his eyes was enough for

44

Rand, told him what he wanted to know. He smiled thinly.

"That's news, huh, Boicer? I've been wondering why Fat said he got it from Iswell that I'm Ringer Barran. Fat didn't get it from you because you didn't know. Isn't that right, Boicer?"

"I wasn't knowin' that you're Ringer Barran," admitted the sheriff in a choked voice.

"Iswell's been here, told me *he* knew," Rand said grimly. "Kind of queer he didn't tell *you* what he knew about me." He fumbled in the sheriff's hip-pocket, drew out a large yellow silk handkerchief and expertly adjusted the gag.

"I don't know how long you'll have to keep company with your jailer here," he chuckled. "Maybe you'll get out when the moon is down and then you can talk over this Barran thing with Iswell. You ought to ask him about it, Boicer . . . ask him why he didn't tell you that I'm Ringer Barran."

The cell door closed gently, the key turned in the lock.

Once more Rand made a careful reconnaissance of the moonlit night. The sounds of a tinny piano reached up the slope from the saloon. Several riders drifted along the street below the jail. He continued to wait, ears and eyes alert. Satisfied at last, he stepped through the door, locked it with one of the keys on the ring and slipped stealthily into the covering junipers.

He came to a tangle of brush and paused for a few moments to rid himself of the jail keys and the gunny sack of cartridges. It would be a long time, if ever, before Fat Wiler saw them again.

A big kerosene lantern swung in front of the livery barn. Rand halted again in the concealing shadows of a juniper. The man standing just inside the wide door of the barn was Abel Gregg. A careful scrutiny of the street told Rand the way was clear. A few quick strides brought him into the covering darkness of the barn.

"Well, son — you done it." Abel's tone was placid. With a gesture for Rand to follow, he led the way to a stall at the far end of the stable. The buckskin's head turned in an inquisitive look. "Figgered you'd be along right soon and had Pablo throw on your saddle," Abel said with his slow smile. He looked at Rand with bright, questioning eyes.

"Nobody on my trail yet," Rand assured him. "Left Boicer and Fat locked up in the cell they picked for me," he added nonchalantly.

"You've got me guessin' plenty," Abel said. "Ain't asking questions right now, son. You have a lot on your mind."

Rand shrugged, looked at him thoughtfully. "You found that piece of paper under the silver plate of my gun, Abel?"

"Sure I found it, and done what it said for me to do."

"Just what did you do?" Rand asked with a grin.

"Sent a feller ridin' for Las Cruces to put a message on the telegraph." Abel shook his head regretfully. "Be another twenty-four hours before Oliphant gets that wire, son. Too bad. Plenty can happen in a lot less than twenty-four hours."

46

"Can't be helped." Rand shrugged again. "Have you seen Benita Ellison?"

"She promised to wait in her room at the hotel till she'd heard from me," Abel replied. A hint of anxiety shadowed his face. "You spilled somethin' back there in the jail, son. You said it was on her account you was in Palo Pinto."

"That's right." Rand spoke soberly. "Her father and my father were friends, back in the old days."

Abel's hands came together in a hard slap that sent a quiver through the buckskin horse. He said with more show of excitement than Rand had yet seen in him, "I'm a damn fool for not guessin' right off when you spoke your name back there in the flats. You mean you're son to Jeff Kenzie."

"That's right," Rand said again.

"I knowed Jeff Kenzie when him and Ben Ellison were prodding cows up the old Western Trail," Abel's voice was reminiscent, his eyes warm as he looked at the younger man. "Them was the days, son. Sure would like to see Jeff ag'in and talk them times over."

"He's dead," Rand told him quietly. "More than a year ago."

Abel was silent for a long moment, and when he finally spoke it was with the voice of a man who philosophically accepts the bad with the good. "Your dad lived a plenty while he lived," he said simply. He shook his head. "I reckon it's more'n twenty years since I seen Jeff Kenzie."

"It's like this," Rand continued, "Ben Ellison wrote a letter to him several weeks ago. Ben didn't know father was dead. I opened it — and — well that is why I headed for Palo Pinto. Couldn't do anything else, after reading that letter."

"I begin to savvy," muttered Abel. "Ben wrote there was trouble on the prod, huh?"

"You've guessed it." Rand spoke somberly. "I didn't get here fast enough, Abel. I might have prevented the murder of Ben Ellison."

"Well —" Abel's face took on granite lines. "Ben's murder don't end the trouble, son. Trouble is rarin' ugly heads all round that girl of Ben's." He added fervently. "I'm damn glad you've come."

"I've got to lay low until Oliphant gets busy."

"You'll be taking an awful risk, going to that hotel tonight, son," warned Abel. "Why don't you let me get the girl over to the barn here."

Rand pondered the suggestion. A lot of people had witnessed his arrest in front of Doc Smeed's house. He was supposed to be in jail. It would be almost impossible to gain access to the hotel without being recognized. As matters stood he had a leeway of some two hours before his escape was discovered. Iswell had said the attempt to break him out of jail would be when the moon was down.

The thought of the surprise awaiting the lawyer twisted his lips in a fleeting sardonic grin. Iswell was due for a shock when he found the sheriff and the jailer handcuffed and gagged in the cell.

Rand's face hardened again as his active mind attacked the mystery of Iswell's eagerness to break him out of jail. The lawyer pretended to believe that he was

48

Ringer Barran. The thing smelled to high heaven. If Iswell knew the notorious outlaw he also knew that Rand was not Ringer Barran.

A picture leaped to his mind . . . the grating jerked from the cell window, himself crawling through, shadowy forms outside in the night . . . gun-flashes stabbing the darkness . . . hot bullets smashing into his body . . . the supposed Ringer Barran slain in an attempt to break out of jail.

Abel Gregg looked at him curiously, wondered at the cold rage in his blue eyes. "Something has hit you hard, huh?" He spoke softly. "You've cracked a tough nut, huh?"

"Yes," Rand answered. "I've cracked a nut. I'm beginning to savvy why Iswell wants to break me out of that jail."

"Iswell is some foxy, son," Abel commented dryly.

"He's a damn wolf," Rand said in a low, furious voice. "He wants to exhibit a dead Ringer Barran and so end the chase after the murderer of Ben Ellison."

"Now why would Lark Iswell be doing that?" wondered Abel.

"It's one of the riddles I'm going to solve," Rand told him with a mirthless smile. He stared for a moment at the old man, his face hard under the faint gleam of the lantern Abel had hung on a peg. "Benita Ellison is not safe in this town," he said.

"She's safe enough at the hotel." Abel cocked surprised eyes at him. "I'm taking her out to the ranch myself in the morning."

"You're taking her to the ranch tonight," Rand insisted. "You are taking her now, before it's too late — before the moon is down."

"You seem awful sure about it." Abel spoke worriedly. "What's the moon got to do with it?"

"Iswell is to put over that jail-break when the moon goes down," Rand told him significantly. "I won't be there in that cell, and that means trouble in carload lobe headed straight for Benita Ellison."

"I don't quite savvy," complained the old man, "but I'd sure go to hell and back to head off trouble from that girl. All right, son. I won't buck the notion." His voice lifted in a low call that brought the muffled thud of running feet.

Pablo Casado slid from, the darkness, halted in the faint light of the lantern. He gave Rand a friendly grin.

"Get the bay team hitched to the buckboard in a hurry, Pablo," ordered Abel. "I'm drivin' Benita over to the ranch."

"*Si!*" Pablo sped away.

"Get her away from the hotel on the quiet," Rand said to Abel. "She mustn't let anybody know she's leaving."

"She's got her trunk up in her room," worried Abel.

"She can let it stay there." Rand's tone was urgent. "You fix it, Abel. Get her over to the barn, and get her out of town on the quiet. Tell Pablo not to answer questions if anybody comes around looking for you. He can say you've gone to bed and that he doesn't know anything about the girl, if he's asked."

"I'll fix it," agreed Abel. "I'll go over to the hotel now, tell her to make a sneak out the back way and head for the barn." His eyes narrowed in a speculative look at the younger man. "Which way are *you* headed for?"

Rand grinned. "The same way as you — for the girl's ranch. You won't see me, but I'll be close."

Abel showed signs of relief. He nodded. "I like the notion," he approved. "If things are as bad as you say, we'll maybe want you awful close."

"Listen." Rand spoke grimly. "Sundown Skaggs took a bullet, up there in Piñon Pass. You said yourself that Sundown was the milk of human kindness . . . you said you couldn't figure who would want to kill him."

"That's gospel truth," agreed Abel. "Don't make sense, anybody wanting to kill old Sundown."

"That bullet wasn't intended for Sundown," Rand said quietly. The conviction in his voice brought a startled grunt from the liveryman. He gave Rand a shocked look. "It was an attempt to kill Benita Ellison," the latter finished.

"By God!" Abel said. Anger deepened his voice. "By God — I believe you've hit on the truth, son."

"It's the only answer." The look of rage was back in his eyes. "You see, Abel, I learned things in that letter Ben Ellison wrote, not knowing my father was dead."

"I'm some muddled in my mind about it," Abel confessed.

"No time now to explain," Rand told him. "Get moving, Abel. Every minute counts."

"I ain't used a gun for a coon's age," the old ex-freighter said in a hard, rasping voice. "I'm bucklin' on that old .45 of mine right now, and I reckon I'll take my Sharps buffalo gun along with me." His eyes gleamed in the lantern light. "That old Sharps has done a heap of killin' in her time, son."

"Down at Gregg's Crossing, huh?" smiled Rand.

"There's worse things than painted Comanches," Abel told him grimly. "A Comanche is a lily-white saint put alongside sneakin', schemin', two-legged humans that plot cold-blooded murder." He jerked Rand a brief nod, turned quickly away.

Rand stood for a long moment, his expression grim with the thoughts that chased through his mind. He heard the low murmur of voices from the front end of the long stable. His hand lowered, fastened over the butt of the gun in his holster. The feel of it under his clenched fingers drew, a frown from him. He had forgotten to ask Abel for the return of his own Colt .45.

He listened intently, eyes fixed down the dark passage that ran behind the stalls. A lantern suddenly came dancing toward him, a man — Pablo Casado.

The Mexican slid up, lantern swinging in one hand, in the other dangled the long barrelled .45 with the silver plate in the butt. "*El señor* say geeve thees gun to you." Pablo's brown face wrinkled in a smile, and he added softly, "Mebbe use heem for keel snakes, no?"

Rand took the Colt with one hand and removed Fat's .45 with the other. "*Muchos gracias*, Pablo." He pushed the recovered gun into its rightful holster and thrust the jailer's weapon inside his shirt. He would have to dispose of it in the brush out of town. It would make trouble for Abel if Fat Wiler chanced to find his confiscated .45 lying around in the barn.

"You speak my tongue?" Pablo spoke in Spanish, a pleased look in his eyes.

"All my life," chuckled Rand. "Sure I speak Spanish."

"Listen." Pablo continued in Spanish. "I would ride with you . . . hunt down the man who killed the father of Benita Ellison." Emotion shook him, his eyes blazed.

"Maybe you will get the chance," Rand told him. He gave the old Mexican a kindly look. "She needs all her friends."

"I am her friend," Pablo declared. "I am old — but I can still fight."

"All right, Pablo." Rand turned to the buckskin. "You keep eyes and ears open. There are things we must learn."

"My eyes and ears will never sleep," promised the Mexican simply.

Rand brought the buckskin horse from the stall. "I must get out of here the back way," he said to Pablo.

The Mexican led him to a small rear door. "Beyond the trees is the bluff," he directed in Spanish. "You will find a trail that follows along the river to the ford. Take the left turn where the road forks beyond the river."

"Adios, amigo." Rand swung into the saddle and in mother moment horse and rider were lost to view in the dark cover of the junipers.

CHAPTER
SIX

Clanton Boicer was perhaps the angriest man in the County of Palo Pinto. He would never hear the last of the indignity he had suffered at the hands of the low down border desperado who had so neatly trussed him up in his own jail. Curious gurgling noises filtered through the yellow silk bandanna that bound his mouth, hot oaths that were choked back in his throat and sent flecks of saliva oozing from the corners of his lips. It was futile to fight against the handcuffs that held his arms behind his back, and it was impossible to get up from the hard mud floor. Ringer Barran, or Rand Kenzie, as the scoundrel chose to call himself, had tied his ankles with the sheriff's own belt and hooked the jailer's booted feet inside the leather loop. Sheriff and jailer were helplessly snagged together in their own bootheels. They could only lie there and splutter unintelligible curses at the whole world and Ringer Barran in particular.

The fretwork of moonlight on the floor slowly dimmed out. Faint sounds reached their straining ears from the pitch blackness outside the window grating. The two men lying prone on the cell floor listened with considerable amazement. Their ears were not deceiving them. Those were footsteps they heard. Prowlers were outside, stealthily approaching the window.

There was a silence, a low whisper of voices, a finger scraped softly across the grating. Another silence, the finger, or several fingers, seemed to be busy with the iron bars. A faint rasping noise, a rope being passed inside and around the iron bars and drawn outside. A low, guarded voice reached the puzzled occupants of the cell.

"All set, feller. Come a-kitin' when them bars bust out."

The speaker's footfalls receded into the night. Sheriff Boicer made strange gurgling sounds. He was attempting to tell Fat what the jailer had already guessed. Fat made similar curious sounds indicating that he damn well knew it was a jail-break and that in his opinion the sheriff talked like a baboon. Fortunately for the jailer his own mouthings were even more unintelligible than the sheriff's.

A quick, harsh rasping drew their attention hard on the window. They recognized the meaning of that sound. The ropes passed around the bars had been drawn taut, ready for the tug that would snap them from the adobe framework.

From the distance came the faint sharp flurry of horses' hoofs digging in for a running start. A rending crack broke the stillness of the night, a dull clang outside as the twisted iron grating struck the ground.

Again a silence, a long silence. The sheriff and his jailer sensed the growing bewilderment outside. Ringer Barran's friends were puzzled.

A low, annoyed voice floated in. "What's keepin' you? We cain't stick 'round here after all that noise we made."

The continued silence from the cell plainly irked the speaker. Something scraped against the outside wall, a faint glow sprang up, followed by a flare of light as a block of sputtering sulphur matches hurtled through the window and struck the floor close to Boicer's head. The sheriff recoiled violently from the flaming matches.

A startled grunt from the window echoed Boicer's alarmed gurgles. The light made by the block of matches had told the man enough. They heard the staccato click of bootheels as he fled.

The night resumed its stillness. The straining ears of the sheriff and his jailer heard no more of the mysterious intruders. Occasional bursts of discordant music floated on the breeze from the Silver Palace, the strumming of guitars from the Mexican quarter. They heard faintly the staccato hammering of hoofs fade into the distance down the street to the accompaniment of shrill yips from the riders. Sheriff Boicer recognized those voices. Some of his own Rafter B men, headed back to the ranch. Muffled curses dribbled from under the yellow silk bandanna that snared his lips. They wouldn't be knowing his plight, but damn them anyway.

A new sound broke sharply against their ears. A banging as of fists hammering on wood, a sudden uproar of excited voices. The sheriff struggled impotently to free his feet from Fat's entangled bootheels, tried to send out an answering shout. The result was a series of gurgles, a smothered anguished protest from the jailer whose ankles were wincing under the crush of the sheriff's own bootheels.

Long moments passed. They heard the sharp crack of a locked door being forcibly opened, the stamp of booted feet in the front office. More loud shouts, another locked door broken open. The corridor filled with light from lanterns in the hands of running men. The sheriff glimpsed the astonished face of Bert Ketcher, staring into the cell, lantern lifted high in his hand.

"My gawd!" The deputy spoke in a shocked voice. "Locked up in the cell — both of 'em."

Sheriff Boicer said something in muffled, unintelligible words. His meaning though, was clear enough. Ketcher replied soothingly, "Sure we'll get you out . . . just as quick as we can find the keys. Looks like Ringer Barran has throwed 'em away some place. Had to break in through the doors."

More smothered profanity from the sheriff. He heard a low, amused laugh from Larkin Iswell. "I'm afraid that Ringer Barran has pulled a fast one on you, Clant." There was a hint of malice in the lawyer's voice.

Bert Ketcher said bruskly. "Somebody go get a sledge hammer. Nothin' to do but smash off this lock."

One of the men hurried away. Iswell spoke again. "Queer business, Bert. I don't see how Barran could have pulled this escape off single-handed." There was genuine bewilderment in his voice, a hint of fear. "He couldn't have got the best of Clant and Fat, locked 'em in the cell and walked out the front door."

"He sure went out the front door," grumbled the deputy. "Them locked doors prove he did. We'll know just as quick as Clant and Fat can talk like humans."

The man returned on the run with the wanted sledge hammer. He attacked the lock and in a few moments the sheriff and the jailer were untangled, helped to their feet and their gags removed.

The sheriff spat, licked chafed lips with the tip of his tongue. "You damn fool." He glared with bloodshot eyes at the jailer. "How come you let him get the jump on you?"

Fat looked like a sick man. His head ached miserably from the crack on his skull. He licked dust-caked lips, shook his head dazedly. "I'm kind of hazy," he mumbled. "Happened awful fast — and I'm sure needin' Doc Smeed." His heavy weight sagged against the man who had helped him to his feet.

"His head is bleeding," Iswell said in his precise, nasal voice.

"I'm dyin'," Fat asserted. He wanted more time to think up a plausible story. "Git me to the doc awful quick."

"Dyin' nothing," Ketcher said *gruffly*. "I seen that whiskey bottle back there in the office when we busted through. You went and got drunk . . . that's what you done, and then you went and let Ringer Barran make a monkey out of you."

"Somebody get these handcuffs off me," broke in Sheriff Boicer angrily. "My wrist is swellin'."

The deputy shook his head gloomily. "That's the hell of it, Clant. That Barran feller has gone and throwed all

58

the keys away some place. We cain't unlock them cuffs. We'e got to cut 'em."

The sheriff swore feelingly, stared with frowning eyes at the window. The others saw for the first time that the grating had been torn loose. Ketcher uttered a startled oath. "I sure don't savvy a-tall," he muttered in a perplexed voice. "How come you and Fat was hawg-tied in here and the doors all locked, if Barran went out through that window?"

"He didn't go through the window," Boicer said bitterly. "Barran was already gone when some fellers come and yanked that grating loose."

They stared at him, too puzzled for words. Only Iswell spoke. "Mysterious," he said softly. "Very mysterious."

Boicer leveled a hard look at him. He was reminded of something. "You're a hell of a feller," he gibed. "Why didn't you tell me he was Ringer Barran? I'd have clamped leg-irons on him."

"I came right over to the jail to tell you," Iswell answered smoothly. "You were gone, Clant. All I could do was to put Fat wise."

"You could have told me down in the street when we passed your office," fumed the sheriff.

"I didn't know the truth then," smiled the lawyer. His voice hardened. "I'm not taking any blame for Ringer Barran slipping out of your hands, Boicer."

"By God!" said the sheriff. He scowled at his deputy. "Let's get these damn cuffs off my wrists." He stamped angrily along the corridor. The others trailed behind, with two men supporting a very sick and woebegone jailer.

The sheriff's face wore a disconsolate look as he gazed around the office. The rifles and six-guns lying on the floor, the emptied cartridge boxes, shrieked the story at him. "The low-down skunk," he groaned.

"The feller didn't miss nothin'," grumbled Bert Ketcher.

"Ringer Barran wouldn't," smiled Larkin Iswell.

"You wait," blustered the sheriff. His face reddened under the taunt. "I'll have him back in this jail in no time." He gave the lawyer a baleful look. "I'm warnin' you to keep quiet about this, Lark." His gaze swept the faces of the other men. "The same goes for all of you," he added.

"You can leave me out," retorted Iswell. His eyes sparkled wickedly. "Miss Ellison won't be so pleased when she hears you've let her father's killer make a fool of you." He strutted through the doorway, was lost in the darkness.

"The little snake," muttered the sheriff. There was a stricken look to him. He rolled nervous eyes at the group of silent listeners.

Bert Ketcher broke the silence. "Sidewinder," he said. "Sidewinder, that's what he is." He spat contemptuously.

"I'll stomp on him," declared the sheriff. Color flowed back into his face. He added furiously, "Somebody go get Ed Giles. He'll have tools in his blacksmith shop that will cut these handcuffs off quick."

A man clattered out, they heard the stamp of his running feet. Boicer looked at the group of men. "I'm swearin' you in as sheriff's posse," he told them. "Get your horses ready, fellers. We're goin' after Ringer Barran."

They heard the quick thud of running feet and a man burst in from the black mantle of the night beyond the door. He came to a standstill, a big-bellied man with a round olive-skinned face too small for the huge neck that rose from thick-muscled shoulders. Beads of sweat mottled his dark face and he was puffing hard.

Sheriff Boicer looked at him questioningly. It was obvious that Tony Silver was in a disturbed frame of mind.

"You should ought to know it queek," Tony said between gulps that sent quivers through his bulging stomach.

"Know what?" grumbled the sheriff.

"That girl — she make sneak away," Tony Silver said with a flap of his hand. "By damn, Clant — she 'ave go and say not'ing to me." The proprietor of the Palo Pinto Hotel wiped his perspiring face with the back of his hand. "She leave the 'otel and say not'ing to nobody."

"The hell you say!" exclaimed Boicer. His face darkened. "Why ain't you stoppin' her?"

Tony Silver's shiny black eyes sparkled resentfully. "She 'ave go before I know she 'ave go, and by damn, I no like you spik to me like dog. I am Tony Silver . . . I own ze Silver Palace Bar . . . I own ze 'otel." The Portuguese's voice crackled with anger. "I gooda man as you in theesa town."

"Sure, sure," quickly mollified the sheriff. "I wasn't jumpin' you about it, Tony."

"W'at ze 'ell!" Tony stared with startled eyes at the sheriff's handcuffed wrists. "I not know you 'ave been arrest!"

"Don't be a fool," growled Boicer. "I'm not arrested." His face reddened.

"You look so funny." The Portuguese grinned. "Fat — 'e 'ave wear the 'andcuff too. By damn, w'at ees ze joke?"

"No joke," grumbled the sheriff. "Ringer Barran busted out of jail, kind of caught me and Fat off guard." He scowled. "Don't you go shootin' off your mouth about this bus'ness, Tony."

"Sure." Tony Silver nodded. "I no say not'ing to nobody. Make pipple laugh for ze beeg joke." His thick lips split in soundless laughter.

The sheriff muttered an imprecation. "How come you know the girl has skipped out?" he asked impatiently. "Who told you?"

"She go out through keetchen where ze cook see her. Cristobal wonder why she go that way and follow for see where she go."

"Where *did* she go? Spill it quick, Tony." Boicer's impatience was at the boiling point.

"She 'ave go to me barn of Abel Gregg," Tony said with another limp flap of his hand.

Boicer's protuberant eyes took on a glazed look. "Is she still there — at the barn?" He put the question worriedly.

Tony shook his bullet head. "Cristobal say she 'ave go weeth Abel Gregg in hees buckboard."

The sheriff stared at him. "Went off with Abel Gregg?"

"You bet." Tony gestured, added in a puzzled voice, "She 'ave leave trunk in room. I no understan', so I come queek for tell you."

"She's headed for the ranch," guessed Boicer. His eyes narrowed thoughtfully. "Seems mighty queer she'd go off on the quiet — leave her trunk behind."

"Looks like she wasn't wantin' it known she was gone," observed Bert Ketcher. "Somethin' smelly about it, Clant."

"You've said it, Bert." The sheriff came to a swift decision. "I'm hog-tied till Ed Giles gets these cuffs knocked off," he said. "I want to know what Abel Gregg is up to with the girl. You fork a horse, Bert . . . Go chase after 'em, but don't let 'em see you. Sure is mighty queer Benita Ellison would sneak off and leave her trunk behind. I want to know the straight of it. Hop to it, Bert . . . and don't let 'em know you're trailin' 'em."

"I savvy," grunted the deputy. He slid into the night.

Sheriff Boicer tugged impotently at his shackled wrists, winced as the steel cut into swollen flesh. "That damn Ringer Barran," he groaned. "I'll sure fix him proper for this."

CHAPTER
SEVEN

Clouds blotted out the starlight. Rand was not sorry. The blackness of the night was to his advantage. Eyes and ears alert, he followed the trail described by Pablo Casado.

Two giant sycamore trees marked Gregg's Crossing. Rand halted the buckskin horse in a growth of scrub and took a long look at the faint glimmer of lights that marked the town. A good mile from the crossing, and by now there should be some sign of Abel Gregg's buck-board.

He strained his ears, picked up the distant clop of hoofs, the whisper of rattling wheels.

The team was moving at a fast pace. Rand held his horse motionless in the deep blackness of the scrub. He wanted to make sure that the approaching vehicle was occupied by Abel and the girl.

In a few moments his keen eyes picked up the vague shape of the buckboard coming slowly down the slope. It was impossible to see more.

Rand checked an impulse to call out, and then suddenly his doubts were settled by the sound of a girl's voice.

"It's so terribly dark," Benita Ellison said. "I would be scared to death of the quicksands if you weren't driving, Abel."

There was a chuckle from the old man. "No trouble — if a feller minds what he's doing," he answered as the team splashed into the water.

Rand waited until sounds told him the buckboard had reached the opposite bank, then rode down to the ford and started across. The buckskin's ears twitched nervously. Rand let him have his head. He trusted Mingo's discretion more than his own vision. The horse moved slowly, cautiously, as if sensing the deadly quicksands that bordered the rockbottom of the crossing. Rand himself could see nothing, only the dark, sullen gleam of the silently flowing river.

The horse began to move with a faster, more assured stride that sent up sprays of water. In front of them Rand could faintly make out the opposite bank — the road.

He halted the horse at the foot of the slope, listened intently. Abel was pushing the team along at a fast trot again. He could hear the staccato rhythmic beat of hoofs, the rattle of wheels.

He followed at an easy lope, came to the fork in the road and swung to the left. Again he halted the horse. He could see nothing of the buckboard in that complete darkness, but he could hear it drawing rapidly into the distance. Also his keen ears picked up another sound from not far behind, down at Gregg's Crossing. A lone horseman, fording the stream.

Rand continued to listen. The rider was heading up the slope, his horse moving fast. Another five minutes would bring him to the fork.

No more splashings came from the ford. Assured now that the approaching horseman was unaccompanied, Rand rode along for another hundred yards and pulled in behind a big clump of greasewood just off the narrow road. He wanted to have a look at this unknown rider, something quite impossible in that darkness.

Rand was down from his horse and running across the road to another big clump of bushes some twenty yards nearer the fork. His fast-working mind had already seized upon a solution to the problem.

He grabbed up a flat slab of rock, about the size of a tin camp plate and an inch thick, stood there in the covering blackness of the bushes, the slab of rock clutched in his hand.

The drumming hoofbeats hushed. Rand guessed that the man had halted to make sure the buckboard had taken the left turn at the fork. His face hardened. No doubting now that this rider was trailing Abel and the girl.

The horseman was showing some caution as he swung into the left fork. His horse was moving at a shuffling walk that made a minimum of sound. Rand suddenly glimpsed a vague shape looming through the blackness. His hand lifted in a powerful heave that sent the slab of rock hurtling across the road to land with a loud crash in the chaparral some fifty paces beyond. Almost instantly red flame flowered from the man on the horse, the crashing report of a gunshot shattered the night's stillness. Following his quickly flung shot at the spot where the rock had landed, the rider swerved his horse sharply behind the thick clump of bushes, close to Rand, motionless, unnoticeable as a tree-stump in that veiling murk of darkness. Smoking gun in hand, the man slid from his saddle.

He muttered an oath, half turned to ease away from something that stuck into his back. The branch of a tree. He felt a hard jab against his spine and was suddenly very still. It was no broken tree stump he had backed into. It was the hard steel barrel of a gun.

"That's right," a voice behind him said. "Keep as you are — and drop that gun."

"Hell! It's you!"

"I'm good at remembering voices, too," Rand drawled. "Are you by any chance chasing me, Mr. Ketcher?"

Bert Ketcher was not any too quick-witted, or he might have given a different answer. "Hell, no," he said. "I wasn't chasin' you." The gun in his hand slipped from his fingers, fell with a soft thud to the ground.

"You were chasing somebody," Rand insisted. His gun bored hard into Ketcher's back. "Who were you chasing?"

The deputy sheriff gulped nervously. He was reluctant to admit that he was trailing Benita Ellison. He reached desperately for a plausible lie. "I was headed for Rafter B — if you've got to know."

"Boicer's outfit?"

"Sure," confirmed Ketcher. "Clant wanted Rick Drone to know he wouldn't be back at the ranch for a day or two. Rick bosses the outfit," he added.

"You're a poor liar," Rand said. There was a threat in his voice.

"There's times when I lie, but this ain't one of 'em," Ketcher spoke sulkily. "I wasn't chasin' you nor nobody. Was headed for Rafter B like I told you."

"You're a liar," repeated Rand. He pressed gun-barrel hard against Ketcher's spine. "Boicer wouldn't be making a messenger boy out of his deputy sheriff tonight. There's been a jail-break, Ketcher."

"I wasn't chasin' you," Ketcher mumbled. "I ain't fool enough to go after Ringer Barran on my lonesome."

"You're getting closer to the truth," Rand encouraged.

Ketcher's slow brain was clicking faster. "Clant was some worried about the Ellison girl," he confided. "She set out for her ranch with old Gregg." The deputy sheriff hesitated. "Clant was scared of trouble if they run into you . . . told me to fork a horse and trail 'em."

"We'll trail them together," Rand said with a low laugh that was quite lacking in mirth.

In a few moments Ketcher was back in his saddle, his hands securely looped to saddle horn. Rand led the horse up the road to the bushes that concealed the buckskin. He swung into the saddle and pushed Mingo to a fast running-walk. Ketcher's horse followed freely at the end of a lead-rope, the frantic deputy sheriff a helpless prisoner in the saddle.

The few minutes' delay had been enough to carry the buckboard beyond hearing. Rand sent the buckskin into a fast lope. Ketcher's horse followed willingly. Muttered curses from the deputy sheriff lifted intermittently above the clattering hoofs.

The road dipped down to a wide sandy waste. Rand brought the horses to a standstill, spoke sharply to the cursing deputy. "Shut up!" In the deep silence that followed he again picked up the distant grind of wheels. His surmise was correct. The road that wound across the sandy waste had been too heavy for fast traveling. The slow pull through the sand drifts had given Rand and Ketcher a chance to make up the lost time.

"How far is it to Rafter B?" Rand asked the deputy.

"Maybe some twelve miles from where we're at," Ketcher replied. "The road forks the other side of Sand Crawl. Goes straight ahead for the Ellison place . . . turns left for Rafter B."

"Sand Crawl?" Rand's tone was thoughtful.

"Sure it's Sand Crawl," asserted Ketcher. "The sands is always on the move, sort of crawls . . . gets awful bad when there's wind — and there's plenty wind most of the time. A hell of a place, them sinks."

"Bad place for a man to be caught on foot on a dark night," Rand commented.

"Hell, yes!" Suspicion was suddenly in the man's voice, a hint of panic. "What's the reason you askin' about it, Barran?"

Rand ignored the question, started the horses down the slope. Sand sucked at shod hoofs, held the horses to a plodding walk. From the pitch blackness ahead of them came the telltale grind of the buckboard's iron-rimmed tires.

Sand lifted in little spurts, slithered across the road that wound between vast dunes. The wind was rising.

Ketcher spoke from the horse that closely followed on the lead-rope, "I'd push along damn fast if I was you, Barran. Awful easy to get lost when the sand flies. Gets so thick a feller cain't breathe."

"How far across?" Rand asked.

"Maybe a couple of miles — if you don't get off the road," Ketcher answered. His growing nervousness was apparent. "Wind's gettin' up awful fast," he added.

The buckskin snorted, shook his head as a dust devil whirled across the road. Rand soothed him with soft-spoken words. Mingo broke into a heavy-footed trot through the clutching sand. Ketcher's horse followed, crowded close to the buckskin's rump as if fearful of being left behind.

The wind increased. Rand could hear the restless sand, slithering, crawling, whipping into the air in long streamers that stung his face. He drew up his bandanna over mouth and nose. Ketcher's disconsolate, terrified voice reached to him through the heavy murk. "I'm chokin' . . . my gawd . . . I cain't get my bandanna up with my hands snagged to the saddle."

Rand felt no pity for him. He was thinking of Benita Ellison. Only the thought of Abel Gregg kept his fears for her in leash. Abel was desert-wise. He would know the dangers of Sand Crawl.

Relief surged through him when his ears suddenly picked up the clean hard clatter of hoofs in the

70

blackness ahead, the rattle of fast-spinning wheels. The buckboard had reached honest ground again and was rapidly increasing its lead.

The buckskin horse plunged doggedly ahead. Rand made no attempt to guide him. He was leaving it to Mingo. There was no more speech from Ketcher. He eat humped over in his saddle, head sunk low over his chest to keep the biting sand from face and eyes. And all around them lifted a sinister hissing, the low moaning of the rising wind.

The buckskin's head went up in a quick toss, hard ground rang under shod hoofs, and they were moving at a fast gallop up a long slope. The horse on the lead-rope raced alongside, head tossing, nostrils blowing gustily.

Rand let them run for a good quarter of a mile, until at last they were well beyond the swirling sand. Again his alert ears picked up the rattle of buckboard wheels ahead.

He pulled the horses to a walk, spoke softly over his shoulder to Ketcher.

"How far to the fork?"

"Should be close," Ketcher answered. "What for you want to know, Barran?" His tone was uneasy.

"I'm sending you home to the Rafter B," Rand told him with a low chuckle. He halted the buckskin. "Looks like the road forks here, Ketcher."

"Sure," said the deputy sheriff, still more uneasily. "The left turn heads for Rafter B."

Rand climbed from his saddle and freed the deputy's hands. Ketcher got stiffly down from the saddle, wiped dust-grimed eyes with his bandanna. "Sure is hell's backyard, that place," he complained.

"Take off your boots," Rand ordered.

Ketcher started to protest. Something menacing in the tall, rigid shape that confronted him brought a halt to his tongue. He could hardly see Rand's face behind the night's black mask, but he read enough there to sense an implacable purpose not to be swerved by words from him. He sat down on a boulder, sulkily tugged feet out of boots.

"Your socks, too," Rand said.

"You're a devil, Barran," snarled the horrified deputy sheriff. "You're settin' me afoot. Only a devil would pull off a trick like that on a feller."

"Who told you I'm Ringer Barran?"

"You busted out of jail . . . left Clant and Fat layin' in the cell with handcuffs on 'em." Ketcher spoke gloomily. "Don't need to be told you're Ringer Barran — after what you done to Clant and Fat."

"Boicer and you didn't know I was Barran when you took me to jail," reminded Rand. "When did you learn different, Ketcher? Was it when you found Boicer and Fat locked up in the cell?"

Ketcher stripped off a sock, dangled it thoughtfully in one hand. "Well — now you ask me, I reckon it was Lark Iswell give me the idea," he replied. "I was in the Silver Palace, waitin' for Clant like he told me to. Lark come in, said somethin' was wrong over to the jail, said somethin' about you bein' Ringer Barran, which sure was news to me." Ketcher stared up at the blur in the darkness that was Rand's face. "That jail-break sure

72

had us puzzled," he went on. "The signs all said you went out the front door, took the keys and throwed 'em away some place. Clant claims some fellers come and tore out the window bars and then beat it away when they saw him and Fat layin' there on the floor."

"Queer business, all right," agreed Rand with a low chuckle.

"You wouldn't have had a chance to break loose if we'd knowed you was Ringer Barran," declared the deputy. "We'd have clapped leg-irons on you."

"Listen, Ketcher —" Rand spoke softly. "Next time you see Iswell you can tell him that I'm not Ringer Barran."

"The hell I will," grumbled Ketcher. Surprise crept into his voice. "You ain't makin' me believe different."

"If I were Ringer Barran, I'd put a dose of lead into you," Rand continued, "or I could have dumped you back there in Sand Crawl. You would have been dead a long time before they found you."

Ketcher was silent for a long moment. "My gawd," he finally muttered, "maybe you're right at that."

"You bet I'm right," Rand said. "I'm giving you a chance to tell Iswell that he's wrong. If I were Ringer Barran you wouldn't have a chance to tell anybody anything."

"My gawd," Ketcher repeated, "meanin' your name really is Rand Kenzie?" His eyes widened in a hard look up at the tall man in front of him.

"Meaning just that," Rand assured him.

Ketcher thought it over, sock swinging back and forth in his hand. "Don't make much difference," he said slowly. "Clant figgers you killed Ben Ellison. He'll get you, Kenzie. Clant won't rest easy till he's got you back in a cell — not after what you done to him and Fat Wiler." He added gruffly, "I'm deputy sheriff, Kenzie. I'm doin' my duty if I get the chance."

"You won't have the chance tonight, Ketcher," chuckled Rand. "You're taking a nice long walk to Rafter B. About eleven or twelve miles from the fork, you said."

"Hell!" Ketcher's hand tightened over his sock. "You ain't makin' me walk barefoot!"

"You've guessed it."

"My gawd — my feet'll be cut to pieces," groaned the deputy. "This here country is choked with the worst damn cactus you ever saw."

"Your feet will get over it in a week or two," Rand told him cheerfully.

Ketcher started to speak, choked down on the words. Rand chuckled. "You were going to say it wouldn't be so bad on the road."

"Bad enough," growled the deputy. "Feet ain't made for walkin'. They're made for stirrups. I've been workin' with cows all my life, till I took this deputy sheriff job with Clant. I just ain't no good off a horse."

"You won't travel by the road," Rand told him with a callous laugh. "Climb back on your saddle, Ketcher. We'll ride a piece before I dump you to make it to Rafter B across country."

"You're worser than Ringer Barran," grumbled Ketcher. He got into his saddle, stuck bare feet through the stirrups. Rand again tied his hands to the pommel.

"Glad you reminded me of the road," he said. "I hadn't thought of it, Ketcher, and I want your walk to be really tough."

"I sure was loco, lettin' Clant talk me into bein' a deputy," groaned Ketcher. "I'll never hear the last of this bus'ness."

Five miles up the road, Rand turned him loose. "You can walk back to the fork," he said, "or you can cut across country. The fork will give you some seventeen miles to walk."

"I cain't walk that far," moaned Ketcher. "It's worser than murder."

"You can cut across country," reminded Rand.

"I'll get lost in them arroyos," Ketcher said hoarsely. "It's so damn dark a feller cain't see the nose on his face. Ain't a star peepin' through them clouds. I'll sure get stuck full of cholla spines."

"It's up to you — cross country or round by the road." Rand's tone was unsympathetic. "You can't get back to town across Sand Crawl, tonight, Ketcher."

"Ain't tryin' it," muttered Ketcher with a shudder. "I ain't loco."

"I'm tying your boots and gun to your saddle," Rand informed him. "You won't have a chance to accuse me of horse-stealing. Is this bronc of yours a Rafter B?"

Ketcher nodded sullenly. "I'd hate to lose that saddle, and them boots cost me plenty."

"I'll turn your horse loose some place up the road," Rand promised. "He'll make his way back to Rafter B. A horse always heads for his own home."

He waited until Ketcher's stumbling figure vanished into the blackness of the chaparral. He could no longer hear the rattle of buckboard wheels, but with this affair finished he could make good time. He would need all the time there was before daylight brought Clanton Boicer nosing out the trail. There were things to talk over with the girl now being hurried back to her ranch in Abel Gregg's buckboard.

CHAPTER
EIGHT

From somewhere in the distance came the baying of hounds, a fierce, wild note out of the pitch blackness of the night. Almost instantly a coyote's answering cry lifted in a banshee wail that brought no response from the hounds. The quick subsidence of their challenging clamor told Rand they had recognized the girl in the buckboard.

A turn in the road brought a faint glimmer of lamplight. Rand slowed the fast-moving buckskin to a walk. Another light appeared, made dancing movements through the darkness. A lantern, in the hands of some person hurrying from the house. Then again the stillness was broken by a renewed uproar from the hounds.

They raced up out of the darkness, huge, menacing shapes that made Rand feel glad that he was not on foot. They were formidable beasts with wolfish, slavering jaws that he saw with some surprise wore clumsy wire muzzles.

The buckskin horse snorted, held steady against the clamorous charge; and having done their duty the three hounds headed back to the ranch house, tails rigidly high, feet pattering in a fast trot.

The lantern light winked out. No sound came from the ranch yard. Rand grinned. Abel Gregg was a wary old-timer. He was taking no chances.

He became aware of tall trees on both sides of the road. The avenue — an open gate, with the faint lamp-glow from the house set back in more trees to the right. He rode through the open gate and drew the buckskin to a halt. The gaunt shapes of the hounds slithered up through the darkness, as silently vanished. He heard a low, guarded voice. "That you, son?"

"Right, first guess," Rand answered. He kept the horse at a standstill, waited for Abel to show himself. A shape detached itself from the shadowy line of corral fence.

"Was some worried about that shot back there on the road," Abel said as he approached. He held a long rifle in lowered hand. "Had to make sure it was you, ridin' in."

Another shape appeared from behind a big tree that towered above a long watering trough. Rand caught the flutter of a girl's skirt, heard Benita Ellison's voice, not quite steady. "We've been dreadfully worried." She came up close to the buckskin, her face a pale oval in the darkness. "I wanted Abel to go back . . . find out what had happened."

"Wasn't good sense," Abel Gregg said. "I had to get you safe to the ranch."

"You did right," Rand approved. He told them of the trick that had resulted in the capture of Bert Ketcher.

"You sure got a fast-action brain, son," Abel's dry voice took on a mirthful note. "I reckon Bert Ketcher is due to have awful sore feet, time he hits Rafter B. He's goin' to be some sick of the deputy sheriff bus'ness."

"He would have killed you," Benita said angrily. "He gets no sympathy from me."

"Mighty glad it turned out all right," Abel continued in his placid voice. "Wasn't sure, though, son, and when the hounds took off up the road just now I figgered it best to have my old Sharps ready."

The lantern reappeared, came dancing toward them. Benita said, "Tomas will take your horse, Mr. Kenzie." At Rand's doubtful glance at the Indian, she added quickly, "You can trust Tomas."

"*Gracias.*" Rand swung from his saddle. "I might need him in a hurry," he said in Spanish to Tomas. "Leave the saddle on him with the girths loosened."

The Indian nodded. He was a short, grizzled-haired man with keen, intelligent eyes. A Navajo, Rand guessed.

"I will put the horse in a safe place," Tomas assured him in good Mission Spanish. "If danger comes, he will be ready."

Abel Gregg's look went to the buckboard. "I should be heading back to town —" His tone was doubtful, and the girl shook her head. "No — you couldn't make it across Sand Crawl tonight. You've got to stay over, Abel."

"Could make it by the long road," Abel speculated.

"No." Benita was firm. "I'd rather you stayed. I'm needing you." Her look went to the Indian. "Put the team in the barn, Tomas."

The two men followed her across the night-shrouded yard to a gate set in a high wall. Rand paused for a look back at Tomas. The Indian's lantern made a warm glow in the blackness and Rand saw that he was unhitching the horses from the buckboard. The buckskin had his nose poked in the water trough.

The gate swung open to the girl's push and they went up a wide, stone-flagged walk. Rand was aware of trees and shrubs, the fragrance of jasmine, the soft splash of a fountain. He guessed that this was the patio, formed by the low wings that extended from the main building at the far end where a woman stood framed in soft yellow lamplight that glowed from an open door. She called out excitedly, ran across the corridor and down the patio walk. "Benita! *Querida mia!*"

"It's all right, Raquel." Benita was running, too, was caught in the older woman's arms. "There wasn't time to let you know," Benita said. "I got homesick, Raquel. I just came."

"It is good," the old Mexican woman said. She looked at Abel with a smile of recognition, gave Rand a politely curious glance. "The old rancho is the best place for you, my child. I am glad you have come home."

"Abel will stay the night with us," Benita told her. "And Mr. Kenzie," she added, smiling at Rand. "You will like Mr. Kenzie, Raquel. He saved my life today."

"*Ave Maria Purisima!*" Raquel spoke in a shocked voice. "You have been in great danger? *Ay Dios Mio!*" She seized Rand's hand, held it to her lips. "You have saved my precious lamb. Always I am your friend — your servant."

"It was nothing." Rand gave her an embarrassed smile.

"Nothing! You say it is nothing to save her life?" The old woman's voice was shrilly indignant.

Abel chuckled, said in his dry voice, "Rand don't mean it that way, Raquel. I reckon he's some bashful."

"*Si!* A brave man does not boast," Raquel quickly agreed. She flung her arms around the girl in a hard hug. "My lamb!"

Benita gently freed herself. "Have you anything to eat in the house?" she asked. "I think our friends are hungry."

"*Si!*" exclaimed Raquel. "There is cold beef — plenty of cold beef. I will make coffee." She bustled into the house with a swish of wide flowing skirts.

"Raquel Perez has looked after me since the day I was born," Benita explained to Rand as she led the way across the wide corridor and through the door.

She stood under the mellow glow of a crystal chandelier that hung from the beamed ceiling of the wide hall, a slim and proud girl, a look of weariness in her dark eyes. She saw Rand's gaze fasten on a portrait that hung with others on the richly aged walls of yellow pine. "My mother," she told him in a low voice. "She died when I was born. Her father was Don Fernando de Ibarra, the great great grandson of the Ibarra who first owned Red Rock Ranch." She smiled faintly. "It was Rancho Piedra Rosa in those days. After father married mother he changed it to Red Rock Ranch."

"You look a lot like your mother," Rand said.

"But she is beautiful," Benita exclaimed with a quick look at the lovely face on the wall.

Rand gave her a grin, followed Abel down the hall. "I reckon it's good sense to wash off some of that dust we picked up crossin' Sand Crawl," the old man was saying. "I'm so full of sand a lizard could feel real at home on me."

It was evident that Abel knew his way about in the rambling old ranchhouse. He conducted Rand to a small wash room where there was a hand pump and several basins on a built-in bench. There were clean towels of rough linen on a shelf and bars of home-made soap. The two men washed hands and faces, and guided by Raquel's summoning voice, made their way to the kitchen, a large room with a hard-packed mud floor and a huge brick range in one corner. Shining copper pans and kettles gleamed on the wall, a long home-made table stood in the center of the room, and high-backed chairs of the same age-mellowed Ponderosa yellow pine, with seats of polished cowhide studded with great brass nails.

Rand guessed that the kitchen was the original log and adobe structure reared by the first Ibarra who had ridden on the great adventure with Onate into the wilds of unknown New Mexico. A king of Spain had rewarded him with the vast domain known as Rancho Piedra Rosa, to be ruled down the long years by haughty Ibarra dons until Fernando's daughter became the wife of a young gringo named Ben Ellison, who came adventuring and stayed for love.

In a dim corner of the old kitchen, under colorful strings of dangling chili peppers, an old man sat in a huge chair. His head lifted in a drowsy look from sunken brown eyes as the two men entered the room. Raquel indicated him with a smiling nod. "My husband," she said in Spanish to Rand. "He has been all his life on this *rancho*, and his fathers before him. All of them chief of vaqueros, but now he is not good for the saddle any more. He sits there in the corner and sleeps and listens — and thinks. He is very old, but he is very smart."

"You bet Francisco is smart," chuckled Abel. He crossed over to the old man, shook his hand warmly. "Want you to meet a friend of mine, Francisco," he said. "Rand Kenzie, and a good scout." Abel's head turned in beckoning look at Rand.

Francisco Perez' deep-set eyes took on a sudden gleam. His long gaunt frame jerked upright. "Kenzie!" His voice was surprisingly rich, held a wondering note. "Kenzie . . . It is a long time since he was here."

"I've never been here before," Rand said as he took the old Mexican's bony brown hand.

"A long time ago," Francisco said. "Before you were born." His grizzled head wagged, his hand went to thick ragged mustache, pulled thoughtfully. "It is the same name," he said. "I do not forget."

"My father," Rand said. "He was a friend of Ben Ellison's. It was he who was here, so long ago."

"*Si*." The sunken brown eyes were very bright. "You look as he did. A good man — a good man." Francisco sank back in his great chair, and for a long moment there was a stillness in the big kitchen. None of them saw Benita, pausing in the doorway. She had made a quick change from her dusty clothes to a short-sleeved dress of some soft black material. There was a breathless look to her as she stood there, lips parted, dark eyes fixed on the little group in the dim corner of the kitchen.

Francisco Perez was speaking, as if to himself, his sonorous voice hardly above a whisper. "I remember this Kenzie . . . I remember his words . . . *if trouble ever comes — remember I am your friend, Ben. Send me word and I will come.*" The old man's head lifted again in that piercing look at Rand. "It is well you have come, son of Kenzie. Trouble holds this *rancho* in a heavy hand."

Raquel spoke briskly from the big range where she was watching a coffee pot. "The food is ready," she told them.

The two men ate liberally of the cold beef and potato salad, flanked by plates of crunchy bread and butter and cups of hot coffee. Benita was not hungry, she protested, but surrendered to the urgings of her old nurse and swallowed down a sandwich.

Rand sensed her weariness. "I hate to keep you up," he said. "It is past midnight."

Benita looked at him over her coffee cup. "Abel says you want to talk to me," she rejoined. She put the cup down, added slowly, "I heard what Francisco said to you."

"He was speaking of my father." Rand hesitated, glanced at the unshaded windows. "I'd rather be in some place where any one outside can't look in." He shrugged, grinned ruefully. "I'm not worrying about Bert Ketcher, but Boicer may be smarter than he seems. I can't take chances — just yet."

"That's right," agreed Abel. "After what you done to Clant Boicer he ain't goin' to set 'round twiddlin' his thumbs."

Benita got out of her chair. Her face had paled. "It was thoughtless of me." Her voice faltered. "We — we'll go to father's office."

She led them into the hall and out to the roofed gallery that ran around three sides of the patio with doors opening into various rooms. Set in the wall above one of the doors was a pair of huge polished horns once carried by a romping longhorn steer.

"All that's left of old Tex," the girl said, noticing Rand's admiring look. "Tex was the ranch pet. Father wouldn't sell him. He must have been twenty years old when he died." She pushed into the office and lit a small lamp fastened to a bracket on the wall above a paper-littered desk. Abel drew the window shades, said in a low voice to Rand, "That other door yonder opens on a path that leads behind the corral fence to the horse barn. High bushes on both sides and a feller can make a quick run from here to the barn without bein' spotted."

Rand nodded. "I savvy." He looked at the girl, gravely watching him from the big office chair. "I take it that Abel has done a bit of talking about me," he said.

"Enough to make me curious," she admitted. "And what I heard old Francisco say makes me even more curious."

"I won't waste time," Rand continued. "I may have to get away from here on the jump." Anger deepened his voice. "Boicer claims I murdered your father."

Benita's sharp exclamation interrupted him. "I don't believe it."

"Well, I didn't murder your father," Rand asserted. "I have never seen Ben Ellison. I don't understand Boicer's game, and I don't know why Iswell claims I'm Ringer Barran."

"That snake!" grunted Abel.

"He's dangerous — father said he was dangerous — and terribly smart." Benita's tone was worried.

"You heard what Francisco Perez said to me," Rand continued. "My name brought a memory back to him — the memory of my father — a promise my father once made."

"Yes," Benita said. "I heard —"

"They were old friends, your father and mine — years ago — before either of us was born."

Abel Gregg nodded. "That's right," he told the girl. "A pair of young hellers they was in them days, Jeff Kenzie and Ben Ellison. Used to see a lot of 'em when they was pushin' cows up the old Western Trail. Fightin' fools they was, afraid of nothin'." He chuckled reminiscently.

"I have never heard father speak of Jeff Kenzie," admitted Benita.

"Ben was not one to talk much," Abel reminded her.

"They went different ways," Rand said. "Ben Ellison found a bride here in New Mexico and settled down.

My father married about the same time and stayed in Texas, down on the Brazos."

"The Tumbling K," Abel told the girl. "Jeff Kenzie sure done well for himself. Biggest outfit on the Brazos."

"You can see how it was with them," Rand went on. "The years drew them apart. My father was here only once, probably about the time your father married Don Fernando's daughter. They knew the old days of comradeship were over and so pledged a lifelong friendship, each promising to call on the other if trouble came. The sort of trouble they had been accustomed to face shoulder to shoulder."

"I see," the girl said softly. Her eyes misted. "They must have been wonderful friends."

"Shortly before your father was —" Rand hesitated, then, his voice hardening, "before your father was *murdered*, he wrote a letter. He had not heard of my father's death, and so I read it." He gave the girl a slow smile that held a hint of grimness. "That is why I came to Palo Pinto." His fingers drew a clasp-knife from a pocket and quickly slicing the stitching in the soft upper leather of his boot, he carefully extracted a tightly folded sheet of paper. "You know your father's writing," he said.

She took the letter he unfolded and looked at it in silence. "Yes." Her voice was not quite steady when she finally spoke. "It is his writing."

"I want Abel to hear it," Rand said quietly.

With an effort she steadied her voice. "Dear Jeff . . . I never thought Old Man Trouble could come on the prod too hard for me to hog-tie single-handed, or get me to sending out a call for help. Right now I'm remembering that promise we gave each other years ago. I wouldn't be reminding you of it, but I'm scared, Jeff . . . Not for myself, but for my girl. There's a lot of crooked play that has me guessing. Been shot at a couple of times from the brush and I'm not knowing when the damn bushwhacker will have better luck. Cutting a long story short I'm asking you come on the jump if anything happens to me. For the sake of my girl, Jeff. There's devil's mischief brewing and I'm scared on her account."

Benita's voice faded into silence. She sat there, the better clenched in her hand. The two men looked at her compassionately.

Rand broke the silence. "I got here as quickly as I could make it," he said. "I was away from the ranch when the letter came, or I'd have been here sooner."

She was making a desperate fight for self-control. Her eyes lowered to the letter in her hand. "Poor father . . . I felt there was something terribly wrong." Her look went to Abel Gregg. "Didn't he say anything to you? He trusted you."

"Ben told me to look out for you if anything happened to him." Abel spoke gloomily. "Didn't exactly say what the trouble was. It's in my mind Ben wasn't knowin' for sure himself. He only knew some feller was tryin' to bushwhack him." The veteran frontiersman scowled under his shag of grizzled brows. "One thing struck me as queer . . . Ben wouldn't talk to Clant Boicer about it. Said Clant was plain no good and that

Lark Iswell was worse." Abel shot a questioning look at Benita.

The girl colored, hesitated. "Father didn't like Mr. Boicer's attentions to me," she said. "And — and he didn't like Mr. Iswell for the same reason." She lifted a disdainful shoulder. "He needn't have worried on that account."

Rand spoke slowly, his voice hard. "One thing is sure. Somebody wanted your father out of the way. We don't know where the thing will stop."

Her face was pale again. "No," she said faintly. "We don't know where it will stop." She added in a low voice, "I'm glad you came. The man who murdered my father must be caught — hanged."

"Right now, Boicer plans to hang me for it," Rand reminded her grimly. "And Iswell claims that I'm Ringer Barran, border desperado and hireling killer."

"Oliphant should have that telegram I sent to Las Cruces to be put on the wire," speculated Abel. "Yes said Oliphant can fix things for you, son."

"He can," agreed Rand. "Oliphant knows who I am and can prove I was a long way from here, when Ben Ellison was shot." He looked thoughtfully at Benita. "Who is your foreman?"

"Tom Lucky," she answered. "I have known him all my life. Tom was born on this ranch."

"He's a good kid," Abel commented. "Some flighty and a bit young for the job. Was all right I reckon while Ben was alive and keepin' an eye on things."

"How about the rest of the outfit?" Rand asked.

"I don't know very much about any of them," Benita admitted. "I trust Tom, though. His father was foreman for years until he — he died."

Rand was quick to notice her hesitation. "What did he die of?"

Abel answered him. "Nobody rightly knows how it happened. Old Tom was found dead under a rock slide up in one of the canyons . . . a couple of months before Ben was murdered. Ben figgered it was an accident and let it go at that."

Rand's grim silence seemed to worry the girl. She looked at him, brows puckered in a tiny frown. "You — think it might not have been an accident?"

"I have an idea that your father began to think it was not an accident," Rand replied cautiously.

The sudden baying of the hounds held them in a thrall of silence. Rand got to his feet, went swiftly to the door. The clamor of the hounds broke more clearly on their ears as he drew the door open. Something else they heard — the distant thud of galloping hoofs.

Rand closed the door, turned and looked at the others. "Somebody coming," he said with a rueful grin. He was already moving to the small side door that Abel had told him opened out on the path that led to the barn. "Time I'm leaving here," he added laconically. He pulled the door open, stared into the black night, then back at Benita who had risen from her chair. "If it's Boicer, do some good lying . . . tell him you haven't seen hide nor hair of me — and please don't let him see that scared look in your eyes, or he won't believe you." The door closed behind him.

90

Abel looked speculatively at the distraught girl. "Best thing for you to do is to get to bed pronto," he said in his placid voice. "You leave Boicer to me — if it's him comin', and I reckon it's nobody else."

She saw the sense in his suggestion, went quickly out to the corridor. "Thank you, Abel." She spoke gratefully, added in a low voice, "I couldn't bear it — if they caught him, Abel."

"They won't," Abel Gregg drawled. "You run along and leave things to him."

"Yes," Benita said. "I — I'll leave things to him." He heard the light patter of her feet as she fled along the *galeria*.

CHAPTER
NINE

With the stealth of a stalking Apache, Rand make his way along the path that Abel had said led to the barn. The path was hard and smooth and straight, hedged on either side with thickly growing tamarisks. His fast-moving feet made less sound than the whispered fall of a leaf. He was anxious not to draw the attention of the sharp-eared hounds. He had meant to ask about those hounds, the reason for the clumsy, home-made muzzles.

The stamp of hoofs came to him from the horse corral, and he caught the vague bulk of the big barn showing above the tamarisks. He slackened his pace, eyes roving for a gate, or a door into the barn.

The baying of the hounds hushed. He could distinctly hear the staccato hoofbeats. A dozen riders at the least, and approaching the ranch yard rapidly. No doubt now about the identity of those horsemen. Sheriff Boicer and his posse. Nobody else would be paying a midnight call on Red Rock Ranch. Something must have put Boicer on the scent. The posse had done some hard riding to arrive on the scene so quickly by way of the long road. Sand Crawl would have made the shorter route impossible. Rand decided there must be another trail across the chaparral, not a wagon-road, but accessible to horsemen. He could think of no other explanation for the sheriff's too-quick and unwelcome appearance.

He found the door. It opened to his push and he dipped inside, was aware of sweet-smelling hay, the crunch of feeding horses. A low nicker came from one of the stalls, the end stall behind which he had come to a standstill. Rand grinned at the buckskin's instant recognition of his presence. He took a step toward the stall, froze to rigid immobility. Another sound, the faint whisper of a voice. "It is you, *señor?*"

Rand grinned again, relaxed his grip on the gun in his holster. "I have come for my horse, Tomas," he answered in Spanish.

A shape emerged from the blackness, pressed close to his side. "My ears are sharp," the Navajo said simply. "I heard you come, saw the door open."

"I must be clumsy," Rand grumbled.

"Not so," Tomas said. "I am Indian . . . I have the ears of an Indian. The fall of a leaf brings a message to me, and the flight of an owl in the night."

"I must ride quickly," Rand told him. He felt in the dark for the saddle, drew the loosened girth tight. "Those hounds, Tomas. They must not give the alarm."

"Their tongues will be still," Tomas promised. "You fear these men that come so fast?" he asked.

"They want to put me in jail," Rand told him laconically.

Tomas showed no dismay at the explanation. "You are her friend," he said simply. "It is enough. I will help."

Rand led the buckskin from the stall. Tomas spoke softly, "One moment . . . I will call the hounds." He disappeared. Rand waited with some impatience, hand gently caressing Mingo's velvety nose. He heard a rustle of pattering feet on straw, saw the hounds closely following the Indian, vague shapes in that darkness.

Low muttered words came from Tomas. The hounds sniffed at Rand's legs, wagged long tails in friendly greeting.

"They will always know you for a friend," Tomas said.

"Why do they wear the muzzles?" Rand inquired curiously.

"For fear of poison," the Navajo replied. "Once we had many hounds, but wicked men poisoned them. All have died save these three."

Rand's curiosity mounted. "When did it happen — this poisoning?"

"Less than a moon ago," Tomas told him. "It was before the master was shot that the hounds were poisoned." He spoke with an emphasis that was not lost on Rand.

"I am here to help fight these wicked men," he said. "All right, Tomas, show me the best way to leave unseen."

The Navajo opened the small side door, motioned into the darkness of the hedge-lined path. "You will come to a deep arroyo," he directed. "There are many places there to hide until the sunlight breaks over the hills."

"I will be back," Rand promised. "My horse is known to those men now in the yard. If he is seen, my presence here will be suspected." He stepped into the saddle and vanished down the black tunnel-like passage between the tamarisks.

The concealing hedge gave way to steep cliffs between which he rode on a downward slope. Voices in the ranch yard broke through the night's stillness. Rand recognized Boicer's strident tones. The sheriff would lose no time in searching the barn for the buckskin horse. He had told Abel Gregg that he would be held responsible for the horse, and would put two and two together. The horse had vanished from Gregg's livery barn, which meant that the escaped prisoner had regained possession of the animal. Boicer would have good reason to believe that Abel was involved. His suspicions would crystallize to a certainty if he found the missing horse in the ranch barn. The law was on the sheriff's side and Abel's arrest would have been the next thing on the cards. As the matter now stood, Abel's presence at Red Rock Ranch was innocent enough. He was spending the night at the ranch because he had driven Benita Ellison home. Boicer could find no fault with *that* explanation. He could only wonder why Benita had chosen to leave the hotel so mysteriously.

The narrow chasm opened into a gorge. Rand drew the horse to a standstill behind a towering mass of slab rock and dismounted. It was not in his mind to go far,

95

only far enough to find a safe hiding place for the buckskin.

He scouted around in the dark, thankful for the faint glimmer of starlight through the cloud-drift. The buckskin followed closely at his heels like a well-trained dog.

The faint sound of trickling water led him to a gigantic upthrust of rock some fifty yards from the trail. He circled around, found himself inside a small, grass-grown enclosure walled by cliffs that rose to twice his own height. A tiny spring bubbled from the base of the tall butte at the entrance which was less than four feet wide.

Rand went feverishly to work, stripped off saddle and bridle and turned the horse loose. He opened the big blade of his jackknife and slashed armfuls of brush which he built into a light barricade across the narrow entrance. In less than ten minutes he was hurrying up the trail on foot. The buckskin was safe enough now from prying eyes, and well supplied with food and water.

As he climbed the steep slope his mind wrestled with Sheriff Boicer's strange assertion that the killer of Ben Ellison owned a black-maned buckskin that apparently was the double of his own Mingo. The sheriff regarded the coincidence as a clue. Rand was inclined to agree with him. Boicer was looking for a man with a black-maned buckskin. So would Rand be looking for such a man. The only difference was the fact that Boicer thought Rand was the man, and Mingo the buckskin.

He was back in the hedge-enclosed path again, moving on soundless feet to the small side door of the office from which he had recently fled. Lamplight made a faint radiance on the curtained window. The rest of the rambling house was in complete darkness.

Voices came to him from the office. Sheriff Boicer's blustering, complaining tones — Abel's slow drawl.

"You're barkin' your nose on the wrong stump, Clant." Impatience rasped Abel's dry voice. "You've looked the stable over from hayloft down for that buckskin. You didn't find him because this Barran hombre ain't here. I'm tellin' you the gospel truth — this Ringer Barran feller ain't been here. I'm sure sick of your fool talk."

"I told you I was holding you responsible for that buckskin horse." The sheriff's voice was belligerent.

"Sure you've told me," rasped Abel. "Told me a couple of dozen times. Why don't you learn a new tune. I wasn't there at the barn . . . I was out on the road, headed for the ranch here with Benita Ellison. Wouldn't be no trick for Ringer Barran to get his horse from the barn — not after what he done to you and Fat Wiler." Abel laughed unpleasantly.

"I ain't wastin' time arrestin' him next time I see him," Boicer said in a furious voice. "I'm fillin' the jasper with lead."

"The law don't commit murder," reproved Abel. "At that, Barran is most likely headed for the border by now." There was a prolonged yawn, followed by Abel's voice. He spoke irritably. "I ain't sittin' up all night listenin' to you bawl, Clant. I'm headed for that bed Benita's had fixed up for me."

"I want to see her," Boicer grumbled. "I'm wantin' to know why she skipped out of town the way she did — leavin' her trunk at the hotel." Suspicion oozed in his heavy voice. "The thing smells bad, and there's something else smells bad. I sent Bert Ketcher to trail after you. Was worried you'd run into Barran. Bert ain't here and I want to know where he's went."

"You make me sick," complained Abel. "I don't keep track of your pups." He paused, added significantly, "Wind started to blow like hell when we come over Sand Crawl. You know what Sand Crawl can do to a feller when the sand blows, Clant."

"By God!" The sheriff was obviously startled. He well knew the deadly possibilities of Sand Crawl. "Bert wouldn't have a chance in that damn sink hole on a night like this. Let's ride, boys. If Bert is in Sand Crawl he's needin' help."

There was a clatter of bootheels, the scrape and jingle of spurs as the sheriff and his posse surged out to the corridor. Rand grinned to himself in the darkness, called blessings down on the old ex-bullwhacker.

Voices came from the ranch yard, the quick rush of trampling hoofs as the posse spurred away.

Rand gently eased the little door open, stepped into the dimly-lighted office. Abel looked at him from his chair, his face singularly lacking any show of surprise.

"Figgered you'd be back, son." His tone was laconic.

"I had to get that buck horse of mine out of sight," smiled Rand. He drew tobacco and papers from his shirt pocket. "Smart work, Abel. That talk about Ketcher being in Sand Crawl got Boicer's mind off seeing Miss Ellison."

Abel Gregg chuckled. "I figgered he'd take the bait." His face hardened. "Boicer sure picked up your trail awful fast, son."

"Meaning what?" Rand touched a match to his cigarette, sent a keen look at the old man in the chair.

"Meanin' you was seen leaving town."

"I don't see how." Rand was skeptical. "Pablo Casado put me on the trail back of your barn, and it was as dark as pitch."

"I was thinkin' of Lark Iswell," Abel said with an ominous shake of his head. "Iswell is mixed up in this bus'ness . . . That jail-break proves it. He was fixin' to kill you when you climbed through the cell window. His plan failed because you was a jump ahead of him figgerin' what he was up to."

Rand nodded. "It was a trap," he agreed. "No doubt about that."

"Folks figger I'm kind of old and useless," Abel went on with a dry smile. "I sit there in that chair of mine in front of the barn, kind of dozin' and actin' like I don't see nothing." He chuckled. "I see a heap of things that would surprise Iswell."

"I want to know all you can tell me about him." Rand's tone was grim.

"Sam Bleeker — he runs the store — is awful thick with Iswell," Abel told him. "And there's Fred Craler, a fox-faced kid that works for Sam . . . he's over at Iswell's office a lot. The kid is as cunning as a coyote."

Abel paused, added slowly, "It's my notion it was Fred Craler seen your getaway from the barn. He'd carry the news to Lark Iswell and I figger it was Lark that gave Clant Boicer the tip." Abel got out of his chair. "Time we both hit the hay, son."

Rand glanced at the cot against the end wall of the office. "I'll bed down here," he decided.

"Plenty beds in the house," Abel told him.

Rand was reluctant to disturb Benita. The cot would do him well enough. "Miss Ellison's had a tough day of it," he said. "I can bunk down here all right, Abel."

"She won't be asleep yet," the old man was sure. "She'll be wantin' to know what took Boicer off so quick." He broke off, swung his head in a look at the door. "I reckon that's her now."

The two men stood listening to the light patter of feet approaching swiftly along the *galeria*. The door opened, framed the girl. She had loosened her hair, which fell dark and lustrous over her shoulders, otherwise was still fully dressed. Her eyes widened as she looked at Rand.

"You wasn't expectin' him back so quick," chuckled Abel.

She shook her head. "Is — is it safe?" She was plainly worried.

"Boicer and his gang lit out for Sand Crawl." Abel's chuckle deepened into a laugh. "I give him the notion he'd maybe find Bert Ketcher layin' there some place."

"It is curious that he got here so quickly," Benita said. "I mean Boicer. I'm frightened — his picking up the trail so soon."

100

"I was tellin' Rand about Fred Craler," Abel told her. "It's my notion Rand was spotted when he made his getaway."

Benita nodded. "I saw Fred Craler with the crowd in front of Dr. Smeed's house," she said. "He tried to talk to me at the hotel, later." She gestured disdainfully. "I can't bear that little sneak." Abruptly she changed the subject, "You must stay here the rest of the night," she said to Rand. "I'll make up a bed for you."

He gestured at the cot. "I can stretch out here."

"No," protested the girl.

"I'd prefer it," Rand insisted. His look went significantly to the little side door. "Easier for me to get away from here if Boicer gets the idea to head back for another look." He explained about the hiding place he had found for the buckskin horse.

Benita saw the wisdom of his plan. She turned to the *galeria* door. "I'll see you in the morning." A smile lurked in her tired eyes. "*Buenas noches*, Rand."

His look covered her, warm, friendly, wiping the hard lines from his face. He answered softly, "*Buenos noches — Benita*."

Abel Gregg chuckled. He seemed pleased for some reason. He went slowly to the door, paused and looked back at Rand. "She likes you, son, and she trusts you," he said. "Ben Ellison will sure rest easy in his grave, knowin' that Jeff Kenzie's son is here on the job." The door closed behind him.

Rand stood there for a long minute, a curious light in his eyes, a half smile relaxing the grim set of his mouth. Slowly his musing gaze traveled around the room,

101

rested for a moment on a silver-mounted saddle that was forked on a padded wall-tree. Ben Ellison's saddle, he guessed. A belt of fine hand-worked leather with holster attached, hung near the saddle. A long-barrelled Colt's .45 was in the holster. On the other side of the saddle were two rifles and a shotgun in a rack, and from the saddle's horn dangled a pair of spurs. All that remained of Benjamin Ellison, cowman, and late owner of Rancho Piedra Rosa, proud heritage of the Ibarras. The gringo husband of Don Fernando's daughter had changed the name to Red Rock Ranch. Ben Ellison was gone, mysteriously murdered. Only these simple things of a cowman's everyday life remained — and the girl who Abel Gregg said had put her trust in a man she had never before seen or heard of.

Rand's face set in hard, implacable lines. He reached out a hand to the lamp, turned down the wick and blew out the light. In another moment the cot creaked under his weight. He was more tired than he knew. So much had happened since he had halted his horse in front of Abel Gregg's livery barn. He was asleep almost instantly, so soundly that he did not awaken when the *galeria* door quietly opened and a slim shape glided soundlessly through the darkness to the cot. A blanket fell softly over the sleeping man, and with a faint smile, Benita tiptoed from the room.

CHAPTER
TEN

Eleven horsemen rode up Palo Pinto's short main street. The early morning sun, blazing over saw-tooth hills, drew iridescent fire from the dust that riffled from clattering hoofs. The riders sagged wearily in their saddles, their faces lined with dust and sweat, their eyes red-rimmed, sullen and gloomy.

Early as it was, Larkin Iswell had breakfasted. He stood on the hotel porch, carefully opening the end of a cigar with the gold toothpick attached to his watch-chain. His eyes widened in an interested look at the oncoming horsemen.

Sheriff Boicer halted his tired horse and climbed stiffly from his saddle. "Been one hell of a night," he said gruffly to the lawyer. His gaze swept the dust-begrimed faces of the posse. "All right, boys. Get your horses put up and head back here to the hotel. You're havin' breakfast on the county."

The possemen rode on up the street, one of them leading the sheriff's horse. Boicer wearily mounted the porch steps, took off his wide-brimmed hat and beat it against his legs. "Got lost in Sand Crawl," he told Iswell. "Been eatin' sand all night."

The lawyer stepped back to avoid the dust that eddied up from the sheriff's leather chaps. Tony Silver appeared from the lobby, curious-eyed and voluble. "W'at ze 'ell 'appen? By damn you look bad."

The sheriff gave him a chilly look. "The boys is eatin' breakfast here, Tony. Have your cook throw plenty steaks on the pan."

"Sure, sure." Tony put his head inside the door, bawled an order to the man behind the desk. With the same breath he flung another question at the sheriff. "How come you go get lost in San' Crawl?"

"We was lookin' for Bert Ketcher," Boicer answered gloomily. He gave his interested listeners a brief account of his futile visit to Red Rock Ranch. "Only one answer," he said. "Bert must have got caught in Sand Crawl, or he'd have been there at the ranch, or some place close."

Larkin Iswell put a match to his neglected cigar, shook his head doubtfully. "Ketcher should know his way around," he commented.

"You wasn't out there in Sand Crawl," rasped the sheriff. "That sink hole is sure hell's back yard when the sand flies. Black as pitch, and we was fools to go lookin' for him. I'm declarin' out loud we was damn lucky to get out ourselves."

Tony Silver nodded sympathetic agreement. "That Ringer Barran 'as go make beeg trouble for you all right," he said.

"I'll get him," promised the sheriff violently. His inflamed eyes took on the glare of an infuriated bull. "I figgered to swing him for killin' Ben Ellison, but this

104

time I'm sure goin' to fill him with lead for what's happened to Bert."

"Tut, tut, sir." The lawyer's tone was caustic. "Do I hear the sheriff of Palo Pinto planning *murder?*"

Boicer started an angry rejoinder, broke off and stamped noisily into the lobby. Tony Silver and Iswell exchanged sly grins. "He ees ze beeg fool," Tony said softly as he turned to follow the sheriff.

Larkin Iswell went on down the steps and crossed the street to his office. At the door he paused, lifted a beckoning hand to the youth swilling water from a bucket over the wide porch of Sam Bleeker's store.

Sam Bleeker, standing in the doorway, also saw the beckoning gesture. "Run over and see what Lark wants, Fred," he said to the youth.

"Shorty Tod is about due to pick up the mail," reminded Fred Craler.

"I'll fix up the mail," Bleeker said. "You go find out what Lark wants. Looks like something is up."

Fred put down his empty bucket, wiped a long black lock of hair from his shifty pale eyes and went slouching down the street.

Iswell gave him a sharp look as he stepped inside the office. "What's the news on Sundown?" he asked.

"Ain't had no chance for a talk with him," Fred replied. He grinned. "That Simmons woman won't let me get to him . . . says Sundown's too sick to see folks."

The lawyer considered him for a long moment. "Mrs. Simmons talk any?" He shook his head, put the question more clearly. "I mean has she said if Sundown saw who it was shot him?"

"She hasn't said nothin' to me," Fred answered.

"Keep at her," the lawyer said. "Have Sam send him ice cream."

"Sure," Fred lighted the cigarette he had twisted into shape. "What's on your mind, Lark?"

"I've a job for you." He knocked the ash from his cigar. "I'm going out to Red Rock Ranch to have a talk with the Ellison girl. I want you to frame up some excuse to be there."

Fred considered for a moment. "That's easy," he finally said. "Some stuff come in for Tom Lucky on the stage last evening. Some saddle gear he had us get for him. I can take it out to the ranch . . . tell 'em I figgered he was in a hurry for the stuff." He gave the lawyer a crafty look. "What do you want me to do, out there?"

"Keep your eyes and ears wide open," Iswell told him. "Abel Gregg drove her home last night —"

Fred interrupted him. "Sure. It was me told you."

"He may still be there, or he may be headed back for town," Iswell continued. "I want to know if Rand Kenzie is hid out at the ranch."

Fred Craler again interrupted. "You said he was Ringer Barran." He gave the other man a sly grin.

"Not to you," snapped Iswell. "You know he isn't Barran."

"Sure I know," grinned the youth. His shifty eyes took on a cold gleam. "What time you goin' to be out there?"

106

"About noon," replied the lawyer. "Naturally you will be asked to stay and eat . . . You'll have plenty of time to get in some spy work."

"If he's hid out there I'll sure pick up his tracks," boasted Fred. "Say — Clant Boicer and them fellers with him sure looked down-in-the-mouth when they got in just now."

"Clant says that Sand Crawl got Bert Ketcher last night," Iswell told him.

"Or this Kenzie feller," grinned Fred. "A feller that could do what he done to Clant and Fat could easy make a fool of Bert Ketcher."

"He's a dangerous man." The lawyer spoke softly, stared with hard bright eyes at the hollow-chested youth. "A very dangerous man . . . and don't you forget it."

Fred Craler's loose lips drew into a tight thin line. There was a feral look about him as he stood there, pale eyes intent on the older man. His hand went with a stealthy, snakelike movement to the front of his shirt, came out with a short-barrelled gun. It was a lightning motion that made Iswell blink his eyes. Craler said in a hard, thin voice. "I pack poison for fellers like him."

Iswell said quickly, "Put that thing away. That's your secret, kid."

"Some day it won't be no secret," Craler boasted. He slid the gun back into its hidden shoulder holster.

"Speaking of poison —" The lawyer's smile was sinister. "You should have another try —"

"Only three of 'em left." Craler's grin' was cruel. "They've rigged up muzzles for 'em, so they can't pick up food. Them hounds don't eat only when they're fed by hand."

"Maybe you can work something out while you're at the ranch today," commented the lawyer. His gesture indicated that the interview was over. "See you later."

"I'll be there," promised Craler. He slouched out to the street.

Iswell unlocked a desk drawer and fished out a large envelope from which he extracted a half sheet of paper. He leaned back in his chair, cigar tilted in the corner of his mouth, and carefully scrutinized the heavily penned lines. It was a hastily written promissory note made out for one thousand dollars and payable to Larkin Iswell on demand. The signature, Ben Ellison, was written in the same bold scrawl.

Iswell's eyes narrowed to slits as he sat there, staring at the note spread before him on the desk. Ben Ellison had come into the office a short time before an assassin struck him down. Ben was needing a thousand dollars in cash that morning. An emergency which gave him no time to send to his bank in Las Cruces. Iswell let him have the money and Ben had personally written out and signed the note. The next day he had met Iswell in the hotel lobby and repaid the money from a roll of bills. Ben was already on his way back to the ranch . . . was in too big a hurry to wait for Iswell to get the note from his office desk. Apparently it slipped his memory, and a few days later Ben Ellison was dead.

The lawyer got to his feet, went to the door, closed and locked it. He returned to the desk and took up a pen. It was the same broad-stubbed pen Ben Ellison had used in filling out and signing the note. Iswell dipped it into the ink — the same bottle of black ink — and bent over the half sheet of paper. He worked slowly, carefully, and there was ample room for the alterations he made. Ben Ellison was a man of the wide open spaces, and his writing was like him.

Satisfied at last, Iswell leaned back in his chair and lighted a fresh cigar, his gaze riveted on the changes he had worked on the half sheet of paper. He was a skillful man with a pen. The change would pass the keenest eyes.

The lawyer's lip lifted in a grimace. He picked up the half sheet of paper, got out of his chair and went into the back room. He opened the door, looked at the rise of bleak hills beyond; then with a cautious glance to right and left, he scooped up a handful of sand and backed into the room. He closed the door, placed the half sheet of paper on the floor and slowly dribbled the sand from his hand over the freshly inked-in figures. He shook the sand back and forth over the paper, and again satisfied went back to his desk and returned the altered note to its envelope which he placed in a pocket of his linen coat.

The stage swept past the office as he stepped into the street. Shorty Tod waved at him from the box seat, voice lifting in a shrill cowboy yell at the mules. Iswell waited for the dust to drift past, then made his way to Gregg's livery barn.

"Abel back?" he asked Pablo.

The Mexican shook his head. "No come." His tone was surly.

"I want my buckboard," Iswell told him curtly. He knew that Pablo did not like him. "Jump to it, hombre. I'm in a hurry."

Pablo cunningly dissembled his private feelings. It was always well to know things. "You go far, Señor?"

"Red Rock Ranch," Iswell replied. "It's a trip I hate, Pablo, but business is business."

"*Si*," agreed the old Mexican. "Eet ees so." He stood a long moment in the wide entrance of the barn, suspicion in his eyes as he watched the lawyer disappear in a haze of dust.

CHAPTER
ELEVEN

Sunlight streamed through the grill work of the balcony window, lay warm fingers across Benita Ellison's face. She came awake with a start that brought her head up from the pillow. Dismay widened her eyes. She sprang from the bed, hastened to the window and took a quick look down in the patio garden. A pigeon strutted under the fountain, paying ardent homage to its apparently indifferent mate. Something else she saw, a man, sitting on the bench on the sunny side of a big china-berry tree. It was a strategic spot Rand Kenzie had chosen. The bushes hid him from the view of anyone who might enter the ranch yard gate. He could see without being himself observed. Benita found herself approving his caution. She drew a little to one side, called down softly, "I'll be out in a few minutes. I'm afraid I overslept —"

His eyes leaped upward, found her, a dimly seen face behind the Spanish grill work. Long gone Ibarra señoritas had looked down into the garden through the same balcony window.

"You were tired," he answered. "No hurry." His smile reached, up to her over the cigarette his fingers were twisting into shape.

The patio gate leading into the big yard clicked. Rand instantly froze to attention, one hand on the holstered gun. From her window Benita saw Abel Gregg push through the gate. Rand saw him, too, drew his hand from gun-butt and went on with his cigarette.

"I'll be right down, Abel," the girl called from her window.

Abel looked up, weather-beaten face creased in a smile.

"*Buenas dias, señorita!* You're lookin' right perked up this mornin'." He added laconically, "I've got to be hittin' the road back to town."

"Please wait," begged the girl. She disappeared. Abel stood on the flagged walk, ruminative gaze on the sun-sprayed fountain. Rand said softly from behind the concealing bushes, "I'm over here, Abel."

Abel repressed a start, went slowly around the bushes and gave the younger man a rueful grin. "Kind of careless of me," he said.

"Why?" Rand put a match to his cigarette.

"You could have got me — if you'd been layin' for me." Abel lowered himself to the bench and reached in his pocket for tobacco. He gnawed off a comfortable chew, added grimly, "Ben Ellison was shot comin' up that walk from the gate."

"Meaning the killer was hiding behind these bushes?" Rand was startled.

"No other place he *could* have been." Abel's grizzled brows drew down in a scowl. "I'm awful worried, son. I kind of wish Benita was back in Santa Fe."

112

"She wouldn't be safe there, if it's her death somebody wants," Rand pointed out.

"That's right," agreed the old man. His jaws worked reflectively for a moment. "Ain't no doubt but what that bullet was meant for her, and not for old Sundown. There'll be another try, son . . . sure as you're born."

"We've got to work fast," Rand said. "What about this Tom Lucky?" he went on. "Is he straight?"

Abel was silent for a brief space. "Old Tom was a square-shooter, a good man with cows. Was here with Ben for years, before young Tom was born."

"You aren't answering my question."

"Well —" Abel hesitated. "I know a good man when I run into him, and I know a good horse. You're askin' me about young Tom Lucky, and my answer is I don't think he rates the way a man should. He takes after his ma, and she wasn't much good — went off with a feller and clean to the bad."

"Ben Ellison must have trusted him," Rand said. "He put him in as foreman, after old Tom was killed in that rock slide."

"Ben was a bit soft-hearted," Abel grumbled. "He thought an awful lot of old Tom. I reckon he figgered he'd give young Tom a chance to make a man of himself. He was on the spot and could keep an eye on things. It's my notion he'd have let young Tom out if he couldn't make the grade. He'd have done his best for the boy."

"How does the rest of the outfit stack up?" Rand asked.

"Three of the best fellers quit . . . didn't set well with 'em — takin' orders from a kid." Abel shook his head. "An outfit goes bad awful fast, son. You know that."

Rand nodded. His face wore a sober look.

"A no-account boss makes a no-account outfit," Abel declared. "It's up to you, son. I'm mighty glad you've come."

Benita made a surprisingly quick appearance. She wore a short dark skirt, a blouse of some soft dark material, and soft leather boots. The weariness had gone from her eyes. There was color in her cheeks.

"Come into the house," she said. "We can talk while I breakfast. Raquel says you have both had your breakfasts."

They followed her into the house. "I'm not in the least hungry," Benita said looking at the tray a young Mexican girl brought in from the kitchen.

She was apparently more hungry than she thought. Raquel Perez smiled approvingly when she came in a few minutes later and looked at the empty plate. "A good appetite keeps up a good heart," she said in Spanish. "A steak you have eaten, a poached egg, an orange and two cups of coffee. And you say you are not hungry!"

"I didn't realize it," Benita laughed. She got out of her chair and gave the old housekeeper a hug. "It is so good to be home, Raquel — and with friends."

The two men stood up. "I've got to get started for town," Abel told the girl as they went out to the *galeria*. "You've heard all that's on my mind about Tom Lucky.

It ain't for me to tell you what to do. I can only say what *I'd* do."

Benita's face clouded. "I hate to think of letting him go," she demurred. "Tom was born on this ranch. It's the only home he's ever known." Her look went questioningly to Rand.

"Abel knows men," he said a bit awkwardly. "I can't advise you — not yet. I haven't met Tom Lucky."

Abel was looking at him with penetrating eyes. He suddenly nodded, said slowly, "I'll tell you this, Benita. Leave it to Rand to handle Tom."

Benita smiled faintly, as if amused by the old man's insistence. "All right," she agreed. "I will leave it to Rand."

"*Bueno.*" Abel snugged the big .45 in his low-slung holster, gave them both his dry smile. "If I pick up news in town I'll get word to you pronto. I've a notion there's snakes crawlin' 'round in Palo Pinto."

"Send word if Sundown is any worse," the girl called after him."

"I'll do that," promised Abel. The gate clicked behind him.

Rand followed Benita into the ranch office. She motioned him to take the big desk chair and found a seat for herself.

"I'm afraid you didn't get much sleep," she said, looking at the cot. "You were up so late, and up so early."

"We get used to going without sleep on a cow range," grinned Rand.

"If only Clanton Boicer would drop this silly hunt for you," Benita said resentfully.

"A day or two more at the most." Rand spoke confidently. "Oliphant will attend to Boicer." The doubt in her eyes made him explain. "Oliphant is United States marshal down in the Brazos country."

She looked relieved. "Clant Boicer would have to believe *him*," she acknowledged.

"It's my idea that Larkin Iswell is more dangerous than Boicer," Rand continued. "That jail-break he framed was a trap to get me killed. He would have identified me as Ringer Barran, which means he actually knows the *real* Ringer Barran."

"It frightens me," Benita said. "Why in the world would Mr. Iswell want to do such a strange thing?"

"It's a mystery I'm going to solve." Rand's eyes were suddenly hard. He abruptly changed the subject, reached for a sheet of paper on the desk. "Give me the names of all the men on the Block R payroll."

"There are only seven of them left," Benita told him. "Three of our best men asked for their time. I think they didn't like Tom Lucky." A tiny frown puckered her smooth brow. "Perhaps that should have been a warning. They were good men — old timers."

Rand scowled down at the sheet of paper. "I don't know." His tone was a bit grim. "Good men had no business quitting the Block R at such a time. They should have stuck to you."

She went down the list, finishing with old Francisco Perez. Rand tucked the piece of paper in a pocket. "You told Tomas to keep it quiet about my presence here?" he asked.

Benita nodded. "You can trust Tomas," she assured him.

"If there is anything wrong with Tom Lucky, or any of the other boys, it is best for them not to know I'm here," Rand said. "Or have ever been seen here." He got to his feet. "I won't be too far away at any time," he went on.

"You will be back tonight?" Her tone was anxious.

"Tonight," he promised. He looked at her thoughtfully. He was recalling what Abel Gregg had said about the murder in the patio. "You should keep a good man on guard at the garden gate," he went on. "Tomas would do."

She sensed his thoughts, went a bit pale. "All right. If you think best."

"I don't want to frighten you." He gave her a concerned look.

"Of course not. I — I understand." Her look went quickly to the office door. A voice said softly from the other side, "*Señorita!*"

"Come in, Tomas." She darted Rand an apprehensive glance.

The Indian stepped inside, gave Rand a warning look. "I keep watch on the road," he said in Spanish. "A man comes in a buckboard, and far behind follows a lone rider."

"Thank you, Tomas." Benita hesitated. "From now on I want you to stand guard near the patio gate."

117

"*Si, Señorita.*" The Indian's eyes gleamed. "I will watch with the eyes of a lynx. No man shall pass and my eyes not see him." He withdrew as silently as he had come.

Benita looked at Rand, saw his hesitation. "You might as well go," she said with a gesture at the little side door. "I'm not afraid to stay alone — not with Tomas watching things."

"I don't think danger will come by way of the road," He hesitated, added uneasily, "I'll stay — if you want."

"I'm going to be very careful," Benita reassured him with a faint smile; "No need to stay. And you must see to your horse."

She held the little side door open for him. He liked the way she stood there, her chin up, her eyes smiling, unafraid. The blood of intrepid Conquistadors was in her, and the equally fearless, adventurous blood of Texas. The heritage of pride and unfaltering courage was hers by right of birth.

"*Adios, amigo,*" she said softly. "*Vaya con Dios esta dia.*"

He strode on his way along the path between the concealing tamarisks, aware of a stirring in his blood, a pleasant feeling of excitement that could have nothing to do with the grim business that had brought him to Red Rock Ranch. He paused where the path dipped down into the arroyo. She was still standing just outside the side door of the office. Her hand lifted in a little parting gesture.

The trail dropped steeply. Rand took his time. He was not quite sure just where he had turned off from it on the preceding night. The pitch blackness had made it impossible to note any guiding landmarks. He only knew that the sound of trickling water had led him to the tiny cliff-girded meadow where he had left the buckskin horse.

His keen eyes studied the trail as he went down. There were places where Mingo's shod hoofs had left scars on the hard rock surface. Rand was a bit disturbed. He paused frequently, brushed the imprints with a tough branch he broke from a buckthorn bush. No sense in leaving "sign" for a smart tracker to pick up.

His alert ears caught the sound of trickling water and he swung from the trail with lengthening stride. The buckskin horse must have sensed his approach. Rand heard a soft nicker of recognition.

He pulled the brush barricade away and stepped inside the little enclosure. The big horse nickered again, pushed velvety nose against his shoulder. Rand looked him over carefully. The horse seemed as fresh as ever after his few hours' rest. The grass was strong and nourishing.

Rand lit a cigarette then took a small, stiff-bristled brush from the rolled-up slicker tied to the back of the saddle. He went over the horse carefully, brushed the pale yellow hide until it gleamed.

He adjusted saddle and bridle, put on the spurs he had left dangling on saddle-horn and started to lead the horse out of the place. The tiny spring at the base of the cliff caught his eye. He shook his head as though impatient at his near-carelessness and unfastening the canteen went to the spring and filled it with the clear cold water.

The trail wound interminably down into the canyon. Rand's eyes roved alertly for the fork Abel Gregg had told him cut off to the left a few hundred yards above the floor of the deep gorge. He had said nothing of his intention to pay a call on the Block R camp on Lobo Mesa. Tom Lucky and the outfit were working cattle there. He wanted a look at the young foreman old Abel so obviously distrusted.

He found the trail, swung to the left. A mile farther upstream it forded the creek and veered to the right in a series of loops up the steep slope.

The climb made the buckskin dig in sharply. Rand was suddenly frowning as he studied the hoof-scarred trail. A lot of riders had passed that way since sunup. The imprints were unmistakably fresh.

He loosened the gun in its holster, pulled the horse to a slow walk.

The trail leveled out across a narrow strip of juniper-covered mesa. Rand halted the horse. The fresh tracks had cut to the left, away from the trail.

He got down from the saddle, moved off from the trail a few yards, eyes intent on the hoof-churned soil. He bent over a small bunch of grass that a hoof had flattened. The blades were slowly lifting.

Rand straightened up, his expression thoughtful. The story was plain enough. Some score riders had swung from the trail within the hour and headed west across the little mesa.

He stood there for a long moment, eyes fixed on the telltale bunch of grass. His expression changed to a rueful grin. Men did not ride unshod horses, not if they could help it. He had been worrying over a bunch of mustangs.

He resumed his saddle and rode on through the junipers. He was possibly wasting his time, but he wanted to be sure they were wild horses. And something else had caught his eye. A fine bluish haze beyond the high ridge toward which the trail led, a haze that might be smoke, and smoke usually indicated a campfire.

A ride of some ten minutes brought him to a high promontory. The buckskin's head went up. Rand watched the nervous motion of ears. The horse had sensed the proximity of the wild bunch. Rand halted, got down from his saddle and tied the buckskin securely to a stout stump well hidden behind a clump of bushes.

He went forward cautiously, stealthy as a stalking Apache. Sounds filtered through the trees, the stamp of hoofs, an occasional snort.

Slowly he crawled, came to a wide ledge fringed by a growth of buckthorn. In another moment he was looking down on a basin-like meadow.

The wind was right, and the herd browsing on the short drying grass failed to detect the presence of the man on the ledge hardly twenty feet above them. Watching the grazing mares with vigilant eyes was a rangy paint stallion with white mane and tail. That he was the proud sultan of this harem was evidenced by the some half dozen colts plentifully splashed with black and red and white markings.

Rand's gaze went on across the meadow to the ridge beyond. The faint bluish haze over there had disappeared. The fact failed to allay his suspicions. The approach of the wild band into the meadow would have given the alarm. The campfire had been hastily extinguished. A small fire of hard, dry twigs made a thin blue smoke and was easily put out. Rand felt reasonably certain that a man, or men, lurked back there on the wooded slopes of the opposite ridge.

A trumpeting challenge from the paint stallion suddenly blasted the stillness of that remote place. The grazing mares lifted heads in rigid attention and Rand saw a strawberry roan stallion break from the scrub and come to a standstill. The big paint horse bugled again and the mares broke into a run, closing up into a compact bunch as they swung in behind their lord and protector.

Another defiant blast tore from the paint stallion's throat. An answering scream came from the intruder. Teeth bared and necks stretched snakily, they reared and struck lightning blows.

A flash of color caught Rand's eyes as he lay there behind the cover of buckthorn, drew his attention from the battling horses. The little band of mares had halted almost directly below the ledge. The one that riveted his gaze was a fine-looking buckskin with a black mane and tail.

Rand's eyes narrowed as he stared down at the mare, some twenty feet below him and perhaps as much more from the ledge. Close enough for him to make out the saddle galls on her pale gold back. The mare had been ridden recently, from the looks of those still unhealed scars.

Apparently the buckskin wore no brand. The only visible marks were the sores on her back, proof that the man who had ridden her had small consideration for a horse.

A startled snort from a watchful old mare broke the fighting stallions apart. In an instant the wild band went stampeding across the meadow and disappeared into the chaparral.

Rand remained motionless behind the concealing bushes, listening until the muffled rumble of drumming hoofs faded into the distance. He was curious to learn what had caused the alarm. It was possible the changing wind had carried a warning of his presence. He was not satisfied with this answer. The old mare's upflung head had been turned in the opposite direction — toward the wooded slope across the meadow.

He was not kept in suspense long. Something moved over there. Rand flattened behind the buckthorn bush. A lone horseman. He was not mistaken. That thin bluish haze had been smoke from a campfire.

CHAPTER
TWELVE

The rider came on at a jog trot across the meadow. It was apparent that he was headed for the trail below the bluff where Rand lay concealed on the brush-grown ledge.

Rand loosened the gun in his holster. There was just a chance that he himself may have been under observation. Hardly probable. The stranger's careless slouch in the saddle, his idling gaze, showed that he was entirely unsuspecting.

He came on full-face toward Rand. A big man with a wide, thin-lipped mouth set in a granite-hard brown face. He wore an orange-colored bandanna, and a low-crowned black hat held in place with a dangling chinstrap. The wide brim of his hat was slightly torn. His dusty black trousers were encased in brush-scarred bat-wing chaps and large white buttons decorated his dark blue shirt. A rifle peeped from saddle boot and he wore two gun-filled holsters.

Rand's eyes narrowed as he absorbed the details of the man's look and equipment. There was something deadly about him. He read ruthlessness and cruelty in that hard slit of a mouth, a craftiness in the restless eyes.

The lone rider swung toward the trail. He was less than fifty feet away now. Rand was conscious of a curious shock as he glimpsed the brand on the good-looking bay gelding. The Ellison Block R!

He continued to watch until the lone rider disappeared around the promontory. His curiosity mounted, crystallized into a determination to follow the man. He wanted to know why he was riding a Block R horse. It was possible he was on the Ellison payroll. Rand was inclined to doubt it. The signs pointed to a secret hideout somewhere in those rugged hills from which he had appeared.

For a brief space Rand toyed with the idea of making a search for the stranger's camp. He dropped it. The camp could wait. It was more important to follow the man.

He made a cautious reconnaissance. The rider was already lost to view in the thick growth of junipers, but the lifting dust told Rand what he wanted to know. The way was open for him to return to his own concealed horse.

He rode slowly, content to keep the dust haze in view. Somewhat to his surprise the man swung into the trail Rand had left earlier to follow the band of wild horses. It was the trail to Lobo Mesa, where the Block R men were working cattle.

Rand halted the buckskin at the fork. The trail ran fairly straight for over a mile. He dared not risk a backward look from the man ahead. He lighted a cigarette, sat there on his saddle thinking the thing out. The man was riding a Block R horse — was apparently headed for the outfit's camp on Lobo Mesa. Nothing really wrong with *that* picture, providing he were a Block R man. This was Block R range — where men on the Ellison payroll had a right to be.

The mystery baffled Rand, annoyed him. Instinctively he knew there was something wrong. The man was not one of the outfit, despite the brand on the horse he rode. Rand felt that a man of so formidable and sinister an aspect would have been too outstanding to have escaped Abel Gregg's mention. Benita Ellison would have spoken of him when naming the men on the Block R payroll. She had, at his request, given somewhat vague descriptions of them. None in any way fitted the hard-faced stranger whose dust he was watching fade into the distance.

Entangled in the mystery was something else, something that Rand found himself going back to again and again. The buckskin mare running with the wild bunch. A buckskin with a black mane and tail. The mare could easily be mistaken for his own Mingo at a distance. Sheriff Boicer claimed that the murderer of Ben Ellison had been seen riding a similar buckskin. He had jailed Rand because Mingo answered the description. According to the sheriff, none of the ranchers around owned such a horse. A fact that the sheriff regarded as conclusive proof of Rand's guilt.

Rand stared absently at the disappearing dust haze. He was hardly conscious of what he saw. His mind was clicking at top speed. *The buckskin, running with the wild bunch . . . no brand . . . fresh saddle galls that*

126

showed recent hard and ruthless riding. The same buckskin ridden by the killer of Ben Ellison.

Rand straightened up with a jerk. He drew in a long breath, let it out, nodded grimly. There was no other answer. The killer of Ben Ellison had roped the buckskin mare from the wild bunch, broken her to saddle. After the murder he had turned her back to the wild bunch. She wore no man's brand. No proof could be brought against him that he had ever owned or ridden her. He would know the story going the rounds. The murderer of Ben Ellison had been riding a golden buckskin with a black mane and tail, an animal so distinctively marked that Sheriff Boicer was able to say that none of the ranchers owned such a horse.

It was an answer that left Rand still groping for other answers. Larkin Iswell . . . the lawyer's curious assertion that Rand was the notorious Ringer Barran.

Rand's eyes took on a cold light. He was sure of one more answer. The hard-faced stranger on the trail ahead was Ringer Barran. It was Ringer Barran who had caught up the buckskin from the wild bunch, used her and then turned her loose when continued possession would have been too dangerous.

He snubbed the fire from his cigarette and tossed the stub aside. The dust haze had quite disappeared. He was not disturbed. No need to cling to Ringer Barran's heels too closely.

The buckskin rocked along at a fast shuffling walk. Rand's eyes roved alertly. The man in front of him was both cunning and fearless, according to the stories he had heard. He was a man who would watch back-trail, take stock of any telltale dust. Ringer Barran's life and liberty depended on eternal vigilance.

Rand recalled what little he knew of the notorious border desperado. A former town marshal who had gone to the bad, a cow thief, and a killer. His appearance in the Palo Pinto country could mean only one thing. He was planning a new series of depredations. He would have small trouble in organizing a gang — men selected from the various cow outfits, discontented riders who yearned for more adventurous activities. Such men easily turned to cattle rustling, lured by the talk of big money and plenty of excitement. Abel Gregg had said enough for Rand to suspect that young Tom Lucky might prove malleable material for a clever man like Ringer Barran. He recalled the old man's words, *an outfit goes bad awful fast*.

Rand began to wonder about the other Tom Lucky who had gone to his death under a rock slide. A good man, Abel and Benita had described him. It was because of his long and faithful service that Ben Ellison had wanted old Tom's boy to have a chance to make good as foreman of the Block R.

Old Tom Lucky's death was something to look into, Rand decided grimly. It was possible the foreman's death was not so accidental as it seemed. His removal had been necessary to Ringer Barran's plans; and then had followed the murder of Ben Ellison. It was again possible Ben had suddenly realized that his trust in Tom's boy was misplaced. Ben's letter to Jeff Kenzie was proof he had uncovered sinister activities. He had hinted of fears for his own life, fears fulfilled with tragic swiftness.

One thing was certain. The ugly tentacles of treachery and greed were reaching out for Red Rock Ranch. A dark and diabolical plot that would not stop with one murder, or two murders. Ringer Barran's presence on Block R range was a menace to the safety of Ben Ellison's daughter.

Gloom rode with Rand as the buckskin carried him up a steep slope thinly covered with scraggly piñon trees. Back in his mind lurked the memory of Larkin Iswell's visit to the jail. The lawyer was in some way involved. Rand knew men. He possessed an insight that saw through that dapper mask. Iswell was rotten at the core — a scheming rascal.

Mingo's nervously twitching ears gave warning that he was close to the cattle camp. Rand swung the buckskin from the trail in a detour that carried him into a shallow arroyo.

He left the horse concealed in a thick clump of piñons and worked his way up a boulder-strewn slope to a mass of slab rock that overlooked the camp.

Breathless from the steep climb he lay there for several minutes, studying the scene spread before his eyes.

The signs indicated that Lobo Mesa camp was of considerable importance. The mesa was well grassed and watered by a small creek fringed with willows and alders and cottonwoods.

Rand focused his gaze on the cabin where a man was frying steaks over the nearby fire. He caught the tang of wood smoke and the enticing smell of sizzling meat.

He shifted his gaze to the horse standing near the corral gate. The same bay that Ringer Barren had ridden up the trail. There were other horses in the corral, a dozen or more.

The camp cook suddenly straightened up from the pan on the fire and stared intently into the distance. Rand saw several riders emerge from the trees that fringed the creek. He heard the cook's voice, calling to somebody inside the cabin. A man appeared in the doorway. Rand recognized Barran, wide-brimmed hat tipped back on his head, a cigarette in the corner of his mouth, thumbs hooked over the belt that clamped lean waist.

"Tom an' the boys comin' now," the cook said. His words were plainly audible to Rand less than a hundred yards distant.

Barran stepped outside, stood watching the approaching riders. His confident manner was evidence that he was on familiar terms with the Block R men.

Rand had no difficulty in picking out Tom Lucky. The young foreman of the Block R was decidedly good-looking, tall and lean and blond. He swung from his saddle, stood for a moment, looking at Barran. Even from where he watched the scene, Rand sensed indecision in him, an uneasiness that put a harsh note into his voice.

130

"Hello!" The young foreman's look went briefly to the men off-saddling at the corral. "When did *you* get in?"

Rand's straining ears were unable to catch Barran's reply. He saw Tom Lucky shake his head irresolutely, heard a loud bellow from the cook who was dexterously forking steaks into tin plates that he snatched from a pile on an up-ended box. "Come an' git it or I'll sure throw it away," he bawled.

The Block R foreman said something to the tall outlaw and they moved away from the campfire. Rand's hand went to the gun in his holster. The two men were walking in his direction.

They came to a standstill some fifteen feet away from the low bluff, close enough for Rand to have a good look at Tom Lucky. The foreman's face wore a harassed expression. "I just cain't make up my mind, Jack." His light tenor voice was sullen.

It was apparent that Ringer Barran was using another name in the Palo Pinto country.

"It's a chance you'd be a damn fool not to take." The outlaw's voice was a low rumble that seemed to belong to the barrel chest under his blue flannel shirt. "You said yourself the Ellison girl don't know nothin' about the ranch. You can cut out two or three hundred steers and she wouldn't miss a thousand head if you wanted to send that many down to the border."

"It ain't so easy as all that," Tom demurred. "I ain't so sure of some of the boys. They wouldn't be fooled."

"Get rid of 'em the way you did them three old fellers you was afraid of," suggested Barran.

"Cain't get fellers fired off the payroll *too* fast," protested the young foreman. "It would start talk — get Benita to askin' questions."

"I ain't wastin' too much time with you." Barran's heavy voice took on a threatening note. "You're in too deep to pull off any crawfishin' play."

No answer came from the young foreman. He stared sullenly at the toes of his dusty boots. Rand was aware of a feeling of pity for him, a pity born of contempt. His own code was a stern and rigorous thing. The code of the cattle country, the unwritten law that demanded unswerving loyalty. It was the code of the wild, roaring saga of Cattle, when the southwest was one vast free range.

He heard Barran's rumbling voice, placating now, as if he sensed the younger man's thoughts. "You was born on this ranch, Tom. You've got rights. It was your own dad helped old man Ellison put the Block R on the map. Your dad should have been pardner with Ellison. If you've got guts you'll stand up for your rights."

Tom Lucky's head jerked up in a hard look at the affably smiling outlaw. "Sounds like good sense, Jack." He spoke in a tight voice. "It's a deal."

"I figgered you'd see it my way," Ringer Barran said. His fingers finished shaping a cigarette. He thumbnailed a match and put the flame to the cigarette. "How about tomorrow night?"

The Block R foreman shook his head. "I'm due at the ranch house tonight," he said. "I promised Benita she'd have a tally sheet for the lawyer that's fixin' up the estate for her. This lawyer feller said he'd have to know how many cows the ranch was runnin'. We've been working like hell." His lips curled in a sneer. "She went off to Santa Fe . . . took the easy way . . . left it for me to do the work."

"Sure she did." Ringer Barran's smile was mirthless. "You do the work — and she gets the cows your dad put on the ranch."

"I ain't goin' to be his kind of fool," Tom Lucky said in a thin, high voice.

"You can let her have that tally sheet for the law hombre," Barran continued. "Sure you can." His low laugh was wicked. "You can do your own figurin' on that tally sheet."

"Sure I can," Tom Lucky asserted. "Nobody else but me can do any figurin' on that tally sheet."

"Make it tomorrow night," Barran again urged. "Fix it so the lawyer has got to take your tally. No tellin' but what he'll send somebody to check up on your count. If the cows ain't on the range nobody'll know the difference."

"Sounds like good sense," repeated Tom.

"You don't risk nothin'," Barran told him with a raspy chuckle.

"Ain't so sure about a couple of the boys," complained the foreman.

Barran shrugged heavy shoulders. "Leave 'em to me."

He gave the younger man a thin-lipped smile.

"They're hard nuts, both of 'em," Tom Lucky told him. "Ace Bruff is awful fast with his guns." He added worriedly, "At that — I ain't standin' for — for murder."

"You talk like you wasn't dried behind the ears yet," sneered the outlaw. "Now's the time to get busy, kid. Like as not the Ellison girl will bring her lawyer along with her when she gets back from Santa Fe."

"I shouldn't be surprised none," Tom Lucky said with a scowl. "The Ellison lawyer lives in Sante Fe, a feller named Ignacio Ibarra, some kind of kin to the family — her ma's cousin." He stared thoughtfully off at the camp. "We'll leave it this way, Jack," he went on in the voice of a man who makes an irrevocable decision, "I'll head for the ranch now, as soon as I've got outside of that steak Barbecue's holdin' in his pan for me. Seems to me it'll be a right smart idea to get that tally sheet in the mail."

Barran nodded. "A thousand head short, huh?" His hard raspy voice made Rand's fingers close over the gun in his hand. "She won't never know the difference."

"A thousand short," agreed the foreman. "I ain't goin' to be the damn fool my dad was."

"That's fightin' talk," Barran said approvingly. "Play your cards good, kid, and you'll be as big a cowman as there is in the Palo Pinto."

"I'll have the bunch waitin' at Burnt Wagon Springs," Tom Lucky went on. "Good stuff, Jack, three- and four-year-olds." He paused again, gaze fastened on the group of men at the campfire. "I'll fix it to send Slim Purdy and Ace Bruff over to Paint Canyon to look for strays. Slim and Ace are the two fellers I was telling you I ain't sure about."

"You can count on the rest of 'em?" Barran asked.

"We've done some talkin'," Tom Lucky admitted. He shrugged. "They're all set to go, Jack."

The two men moved slowly back toward the cabin, their voices too low for Rand to catch their words. He continued to watch, anger and contempt in his eyes. He wanted to follow them, an impulse he immediately tossed aside. There were two honest men in the group over there. The others were already tainted with outlawry, resolved to ride the hoot owl trail. To show himself at that moment would only mean the crash of guns, his own life forfeit, and Benita Ellison left helplessly enmeshed in murder and treachery.

One thing was plain. Tom Lucky was not aware of Benita's return to the ranch. The thought twisted Rand's lips in a hard grimace. It was still less than twenty-four hours since he had ridden up to Abel Gregg's big livery barn. A lot had happened since then.

Another thought brought a glazed look to his eyes. It was obvious that Ringer Barran also was ignorant of the girl's presence at the ranch. In which case it could not have been Barran who had lurked in Red Rock Pass to ambush Sundown Skaggs' stage. The shot had wounded the old stage driver, but it was Sundown's passenger the ambusher had intended to kill.

Rand's thoughts raced. Ringer Barran was only one of the pieces in the diabolical puzzle. Somebody had learned that Benita would be on the stage and had sent a killer to get her. Not Ringer Barran. The outlaw did not know she was back. The signs all pointed to Barran as the murderer of Ben Ellison. But the rustler was not working alone. Another and craftier mind was pulling the strings.

Three crows flew in from the creek, circled over the men grouped near the campfire with their heaped-up pans and big tin coffee cups, then made a bee-line for the bluff where Rand crouched in the concealment of the crags. The big black birds fluttered down to a boulder three feet above his head, then rose with noisy flappings of wings and startled raucus cries as they saw the man stretched out below them.

Rand's look went apprehensively to the Block R riders. Their sharp eyes had not missed the crows' sudden alarm. Two of the men sprang to their feet, started running toward the horses at the corral. Ringer Barran took one look over his shoulder and slid from sight behind the cabin. The cook grabbed up a rifle that leaned near the door.

CHAPTER
THIRTEEN

It was no place to linger. Rand dropped from his perch. He heard the vicious whine of a bullet overhead, the sharp, reverberating report of the cook's rifle. He kept on going at full speed, dodging boulders and trees. It was impossible to go away from there quietly. They must have heard the clatter of his bootheels on the loose stones. Loud, excited shouts drifted to his ears, the quick hammering of hoofs. More rifle shots sent out explosive reverberations.

He reached the concealed buckskin, breathless, his heart pounding. He was at a disadvantage, not knowing the country. The Block R men were familiar with the trails, would know their way about in the maze of canyons.

The situation worried him. A quick look showed that the lower reaches of the shallow arroyo offered no way down. The place was an impenetrable tangle of underbrush. It was too risky to head back for the main trail.

What to do was settled for him with startling swiftness. A rider suddenly appeared on the higher slope of the arroyo. Rand glimpsed him only for an instant.

A momentary hush settled over the place. Rand guessed the man was himself listening for any betraying sounds.

A voice broke the silence. "See anythin', Ace?" The speaker was calling from somewhere higher up the arroyo.

"Don't see nothin' an' don't hear nothin'," called back the nearby rider. "I'll take a look for sign down trail."

No reply came from the first speaker. Rand continued to wait by the side of his concealed horse. His ears caught the crackle of brush in the distance, an occasional shout as the chase drew away. Only that remaining lone rider hardly a hundred paces beyond the clump of piñons.

Stillness settled down again. Rand pressed close to the side of his horse, waited tensely for the man's next move. He had gleaned *one* piece of information. It seemed there was a way down the arroyo through the tangle of underbrush.

A stealthy rustle touched his alert ears. His pursuer had dismounted, was moving cautiously toward the clump of piñons that concealed Rand. A short, stocky man, about Rand's own age, swarthy and hard of face. He moved with infinite caution, cold, unwinking eyes probing every bush and boulder. A gun was in lifted hand, a second gun filled one of his two low-slung holsters. There was a formidable look to him, a deadly efficiency.

There was no time for considered planning. Rand knew what he was going to do the instant he saw the man making his stealthy approach.

138

"*Ace!*" He spoke softly, his voice hardly above a hoarse whisper.

The man froze to a standstill, slowly his head turned in a look that met the long barrel of Rand's .45 less than two feet from his eyes.

"Keep awfully quiet," Rand said in the same whispering voice. He stepped from behind the piñon branch. There was shocked incredulity in the Block R man's eyes. Rand was almost sorry for him. "Ease your finger away from that trigger, Ace," he said. "You haven't a chance."

The cowboy's dark face was a mask. His unwinking eyes remained fixed on Rand's face as if in fierce appraisal of his capabilities.

"You haven't a chance," repeated Rand. He added with a bleak smile. "You wouldn't want to take chances for the sake of a skunk like Tom Lucky."

The stocky cowboy broke his silence. "Who the hell are you?" He was careful to keep his voice low.

"I'm taking your guns before we do any talking," Rand said.

The cowboy's clenched hand opened, let the gun thud to the ground. Rand made a lightning reach, jerked the other gun from its holster.

The Block R man spoke again, his voice truculent. "What's your game?"

"I'm taking you back to the ranch," Rand informed him with a grim smile.

"What ranch?"

"Red Rock," Rand replied. "You and I are going to be friends, Ace."

"How come you know my name?" A hint of bewilderment looked from the cowboy's belligerent eyes.

"You're Ace Bruff? Isn't that right?"

"That's right," admitted the Block R rider. "Not that it makes you an' me friends."

"I'm Miss Ellison's friend," Rand said.

"I reckon I'm that, too," Ace Bruff told him harshly.

"Listen to me!" Rand waggled the gun at him. "That's why you are riding back to the ranch with me. Miss Ellison is needing her friends. Savvy?"

"No," grumbled the cowboy. "Talk some more." He hesitated. "You was callin' Tom Lucky a skunk. That's the only thing you've said that I savvy." His lips twisted in a mirthless grin.

"Tom and that man he was talking with just before those crows squawked on me, are planning to frame you and Slim Purdy. I heard their talk." Rand watched the cowboy's eyes intently as he spoke. He saw an interested flicker in their unwinking depths. He asked softly, "Do you know who that man is, Ace?"

"Sure. Jack Fleet. Claims he's prospectin' over in the hills back of Wild Horse Springs. He lost his bronc a week or two ago. Tom loaned him one from the *remuda*."

"Ever hear of Ringer Barran?" Rand queried.

"Sure I have." Ace Bruff's eyes took on a glint. "You mean this Jack Fleet is him?"

"That's what I'm telling you." Rand lowered his gun. The expression on the cowboy's swarthy face reassured him. "I heard him talking to Tom. He told Tom to leave you and Slim Purdy to him if you tried to make trouble."

"What kind of trouble?" Ace Bruff spoke in a tight furious voice.

"Barran wants Tom to send in a short tally on the roundup," Rand explained. "Tom has agreed to have a thousand head waiting for Barran tomorrow night — some place he called Burnt Wagon Springs."

"The damn skunk," muttered Ace. There was shock and dismay in the look he gave Rand, but a singular lack of surprise.

"Tom said he couldn't trust you and Slim Purdy. The other boys are all set to ride with him and Barran. He told Barran he'd get you out of the way . . . send Slim and you over to Paint Canyon to look for strays."

Anger darkened the cowboy's face. "That's what he was sayin' when them crows started us lookin' for you." He stared hard at Rand, his eyes probing, searching, as if wanting to satisfy himself.

"Do you believe me?" Rand found himself liking the grim little man. There was rugged honesty in every inch of his hard-muscled body.

"I reckon I do, after what you said about Paint Canyon. It sure proves you was listenin' to their talk, and —" Ace hesitated. "It fits in with some talk Tom has been givin' me about easy money a feller can make."

Rand nodded, said quietly. "Pick up your gun, Ace."

The cowboy stooped for the fallen Colt. He gave the other man a curious look: "Ain't you takin' a big chance?" A grin flickered across his swarthy face as he pushed the gun into his holster.

Rand held out the other gun with an answering grin. "You may need both of them," he said dryly.

"I don't feel dressed decent without 'em," Ace Bruff commented. He holstered the second long-barrelled Colt with the easy flip of an expert.

"Tom Lucky said you were awfully fast with your guns," Rand said.

"He'll maybe find out he ain't so damn wrong at that," muttered the Block R rider.

Rand looked at the tangle of brush below them. "Let's get away from here, Ace, before your friends come looking for you."

"The trail is tough goin'," Ace told him. "It's the only chance we have to get away without runnin' into them." His face clouded. "I sure wish I could get word to Slim Purdy."

"Too risky," demurred Rand.

Ace stared at him with worried, speculative eyes. "If I don't show up, Tom an' this Barran feller will likely smell a rat," he said. "They'll come chasin' down here an' pick up our sign on the trail."

Rand nodded agreement. The cowboy was right and he found the probabilities displeasing. Ace was watching him intently. "Only one way to fix it," he said softly. "It's up to me to head back to the camp, tell 'em you wasn't down here in the arroyo."

"I'll be trusting you a lot," Rand told him.

142

Ace met his look steadily. "Slim an' me feel the same way about the Ellison girl," he said simply. "We ain't lettin' her down."

"That's all I want to know, Ace." Rand spoke soberly.

The cowboy showed pleasure. "Slim an' me will head for the ranch quick as we can." His voice brightened. "Tom was sendin' us over to Paint Canyon this afternoon. He won't be guessin' we'll make for the ranch 'stead of Paint Canyon."

"Tom is due for a surprise," Rand prophesied. He swung up to his saddle, pleased with the events that had brought two good fighting men to the defence of Benita Ellison.

CHAPTER
FOURTEEN

Vague fears disturbed Benita as she watched Rand Kenzie disappear beyond the shadowing tamarisks. She was aware of an odd loneliness, a sudden impulse to call him back. She turned quickly into the office and closed the little side door, stood there, a hand on the latch, decision darkening her eyes. She was being childish. It was no time to give way to taut nerves.

It was so very still, there in the ranch office. The place spoke of her father. The faint smell of tobacco and saddle leather and gun oil, the littered desk with its stack of tally books — the little things that were a part of Ben Ellison.

She went out to the *galeria*. The garden was empty, or seemed to be. She moved on, along the *galeria*. Her heels made light clicking sounds on the irregular-shaped blocks of red stone cut from the great butte that had given the ranch its name. The walls of the old *casa* he the same rich glow. They had been reared in the days of Don Fernando's grandfather. His *peones* and *Indios* had hewn and hauled the great slabs.

Benita repressed a shiver. She had the odd feeling that the blood of Ibarra men had gone into these walls, given the old stones that warm red glow. *Rancho Piedra*

Ross had seen turbulent times. Ibarras had lived violently and died violently. Indian uprisings and revolutions, fierce raiding Texans — the Yanqui war that had torn the vast territory of New Mexico from the mother country's neglectful misrule.

Don Fernando had come to accept the change with philosophic content. He liked the *Americanos* — was pleased enough to give his daughter to the young gringo who had come adventuring and stayed for love.

Somebody in the house was humming a little love song as she went about her work. One of the girls who helped. Raquel.

> "For the moon I'd give a peso,
> For the sun I'd give a part,
> For lovely Delfinita I'd give
> my life and heart."

"Silly one!" scolded Raquel. "Slim Purdy makes a fool of you with his soft words. He is a good-for-nothing."

There was a silence, then Delfina's offended voice. "Slim Purdy is not a good-for-nothing. He is brave and true and I like the songs he sings to me."

"He sings pretty songs to all the girls," Raquel grumbled. "He will yet make a fool of you." It was plain that the old housekeeper was in an irritable mood.

Benita understood. Raquel was suffering under the same tension that held her own nerves taut. Her apprehensions revived. She was sorry she had let Rand Kenzie leave her. The stillness everywhere frightened

145

her. An unnatural quiet. Nothing stirred in the corrals — the big yard. Tom Lucky and the men were all away, busy with the cattle. There had been no time for her to send word to Tom that she was returning from Santa Fe. He was unaware that she was back at the ranch. Tomas was the only man about the place. There was old Francisco Perez, but Francisco was too weighted with the infirmities of many years to be of any use if trouble came.

She made an effort to reassure herself. Rand had said that danger would not come by way of the road. And Tomas had the eyes of a hawk, the ears of a lynx. From where she had paused in the *galeria* she could see him lounging on the bench behind the bushes, his carbine between knees. He was keeping his promise to watch the patio gate.

Nevertheless, dark forebodings of impending disaster continued to torment her. She could hear the rattle of wheels drawing up the long winding avenue. Whoever it was would soon be in the yard.

She was suddenly running down the long *galeria* and into the house. The wide hall was paneled in yellow Ponderosa pine that nearly two centuries had richly mellowed. Great ax-hewn beams of the same sturdy wood supported the high ceiling from which was suspended a huge crystal chandelier that a long-gone Ibarra had brought from old Spain.

Portraits of haughty Ibarra caballeros and their ladies stared down at the girl as she went swiftly up the stairs to her room. She had the feeling that their eyes were

146

following her with sympathy and understanding. Peril had always been with them in remote *Nuevo Mejico*.

It required only a moment to find the hand-tooled leather gun-belt. Old Francisco Perez had fashioned it for her. He was a skilled worker with leather and the belt had been a birthday gift from him. The efficient-looking little gun in the holster was a present from her father on the same occasion. She buckled the belt around her waist, examined the gun to assure herself it was properly loaded, slid it back into its holster and went across the room to the balcony window.

She had not long to wait. The gate opened, revealed the visitor. Astonishment widened the girl's eyes. Larkin Iswell! He stood there, one hand on the partly-opened gate, hot and dusty — and obviously very frightened.

Benita wanted to laugh. She felt a bit hysterical. She was keyed-up for drama, and here was comedy — at least from her point of view.

The lawyer was seeing it from a different angle. He stared with horrified eyes at the Indian menacing him from the bushes with leveled carbine. The girl's low, amused laugh swung his eyes up in her direction. "It is all right, Tomas," she called. "You can let Mr. Iswell come in."

The Indian lowered the carbine, gave the lawyer a brief nod. Iswell let the gate swing shut, flung its harsh-visaged guard a black look and went up the walk as fast as he could without breaking into an actual run. For the moment there was no strut in him.

Benita hurried downstairs. Raquel met her in the hall. She gave the girl an anxious look. "I do not like him," she said in Spanish. "He is a snake — that one."

"A harmless snake," Benita said with an amused smile. "He looked so funny, Tomas standing there with his gun on him."

Her old nurse shook her head. "Not so harmless," she insisted.

"I'm not afraid of a thing like him," Benita asserted.

"He makes love to you," grumbled the old Mexican woman. "He is worse than that big clumsy sheriff who comes with such loud talk and laughter."

Benita shrugged her trim shoulders. "You needn't worry about either of them. Least of all about Mr. Iswell." She went on toward the hall door.

Raquel stood watching, her expression dubious, then with a quick movement that billowed her full black skirt she vanished through a side door and ran along the *galeria* to the kitchen.

Iswell attempted a jocular smile when the girl opened the door. "What's the idea of the guard?" he asked. His eyes darted uneasy looks up and down the long *galeria*. "That Indian scared the life out of me."

Benita smiled sympathetically. "You want to see me, Mr. Iswell?" She motioned to the porch chairs. "We can sit out here where it's cool." She seated herself, gestured for him to take the opposite chair.

The lawyer removed his long dust coat and sat down. "You haven't answered my question," he reminded with another toothy grimace. His back was to the garden and he craned his head in a significant look in the direction of the bushes that concealed Tomas. "One might think you expected trouble."

The smile left her face. "My father was murdered in this garden, Mr. Iswell," she reminded coldly.

"I was thoughtless," Iswell hastened to say. He shook his head sadly. "Dreadful business."

"It is very lonesome out here," Benita said. "Yes can't blame me for feeling nervous."

He was watching her intently. "Naturally," he agreed. "Ringer Barran's escape from jail makes a serious problem for you, Miss Benita. You are wise to take every precaution. The man is a dangerous killer."

She pretended ignorance. "Ringer Barran?" She gestured impatiently. "Oh, you mean the man Sheriff Boicer is looking for?"

"Clant was very sure the man had ridden in this direction," the lawyer told her. "The thought alarms me. You should not remain here without protection."

Benita gestured again. "I am as safe here as anywhere." The suspicion in his sharp eyes was disturbing, sent a thrill of fear through her.

Iswell seemed to sense her alarm. "Clant Boicer thinks Barran is somewhere near this place," he lied smoothly. "You see, Miss Benita, he passed himself off to you as Rand Kenzie, in fact perhaps won your confidence by saving your life." The lawyer paused, added softly, "Clant thinks he has good reason to believe you may be sheltering the man."

"Clanton Boicer must be crazy." Benita forced an amused smile.

"You can't blame him." Iswell was looking at her steadily. "Remember, Miss Benita — Ringer Barran is the murderer of your father."

"I certainly wouldn't protect the murderer of my father," retorted the girl. "Don't be absurd."

"Of course you wouldn't," Iswell hurriedly placated. "Clant Boicer is a fool. Nevertheless there were one or two things that seemed rather strange. Your curious disappearance from the hotel about the time of Barran's escape from jail. Almost a flight on your part — leaving your baggage behind and no word to anybody."

She stared at him, the color gone from her face. The malignant look in his eyes frightened her. "I'll thank the sheriff to mind his own business." Anger and fear made her voice thin. "You can do the same, Mr. Iswell."

"Quite right," he declared. "I only thought you might be interested."

"I'm not." Her eyes sparkled with resentment. "Is *that* all that brings you out to the ranch?"

Iswell smilingly shook his head. "Quite another matter — in fact a most personal matter, my dear Miss Benita." He leaned toward her, hands on his knees. "You are in my mind very much these days."

Benita looked at him doubtfully. She was recalling Rand Kenzie's account of Larkin Iswell's visit to the jail. Rand had been so sure the man had planned to have him murdered if he had tried to escape through the cell window. She was all wrong about Larkin Iswell. He was dangerous — and there was danger in this visit. He was up to mischief.

150

She managed a polite, questioning smile. "I can't imagine what you mean —"

"No?" His tone was reproachful, his look languorous. "I rather thought you had guessed my feelings toward you — Benita." He broke off, turned his head in a startled look into the garden.

Benita was already staring with surprised eyes at the little procession approaching along the *galeria* from the kitchen. Old Francisco Perez, sitting in the cumbersome wheel-chair Tomas had made for him. The two Mexican girls were trundling it into the garden, and behind them followed a very voluble Raquel.

"Easy, easy!" scolded the old woman. "Would you shake his bones to pieces! *Por Dios!* These wheels groan like lost souls!"

With rattles and bangs the girls brought the huge wheel-chair to rest under the shade of a chinaberry tree. Old Francisco's head lifted in a toothless grin at Benita. Across his knees lay a double-barrelled shotgun.

A curious expression flickered over Larkin Iswell's face. It came and went like a fleeting shadow, a hint of snarling lips and venom-filled eyes that sent a chill-through the girl opposite him. She forced an indulgent smile. "Francisco likes to get out into the garden," she said.

Raquel nodded from where she stood by the wheel-chair. "Francisco make beeg swear he weel get the bad snake. He breeng gun to keel bad snake that c-crawl in thees garden." She patted her husband's shoulder affectionately. "Francisco keel bad r-rattler for sure."

It was the first time that Benita had heard of any rattlesnakes in the patio. She managed to hide her surprise. She also managed to send Raquel a fleeting and and understanding look. She knew what kind of rattlesnake Raquel had in mind.

"Thank you, Francisco," she called to the old man. She gave the lawyer a cold little smile. "Francisco is a wonderful shot. He never misses a rattler."

"I keel heem r-rattler," Francisco said in a deep rumbling voice. "You bet I keel queek!" His roving gaze rested briefly in a curiously intent stare at the lawyer.

Benita was wishing Iswell would finish his business and go. If he stayed much longer hospitality would demand that she invite him for the midday meal. She looked at him inquiringly, tapped an impatient little foot.

Iswell's gaze came back to her. There was an odd tightness about his mouth and she saw that he was staring at the gun in her belt. She gave him a brief smile that held a hint of malice. "I can shoot off a snake's head at ten yards." She pretended to shudder. "I can't bear the things in my garden."

"Nasty things," agreed the lawyer. "Especially in one's garden — an unsuspected menace."

Benita regarded him thoughtfully. "There are worse things than a rattlesnake," she observed. "Father used to say that a rattlesnake was a gentleman, compared to some men he knew. A rattlesnake gives warning."

"Ringer Barran doesn't give warning." Iswell's tone was significant. "Please believe me — Benita — you are in danger as long as that man remains loose. I want to

152

help you." He gestured at Francisco. "All these precautions are useless against a killer like Barran."

She shrugged her shoulders, waited for him to continue. He leaned toward her. "I was about to say something, Benita." His tone was lover-like, almost pleading. "I want to protect you, and — well — to come to the point — I want you to marry me immediately. You need a husband's protection — and wise counsel."

Benita restrained an impulse to laugh in his face. The thing was too ridiculous. She shook her head. "I'm sorry —"

"I'm a lawyer," Iswell continued with a gesture for her attention. "I state the facts with simple brevity. In short, *Benita* — I feel a deep affection for you. I can give you the help you need in straightening out the affairs of this big ranch."

Something in his voice sent cold prickles chasing down her back. "The ranch is all right," she said sharply.

He leaned back in his chair. "No." His tone was grave, tinged with regret. "Not all right, my dear girl."

"I don't know what you mean." Benita stared at him, puzzled, vaguely apprehensive.

Iswell got to his feet, stood looking down at her. "I've been telling you that I love you," he said in a low, passionate voice. "I am asking you to be my wife. Together — we can defy all the dangers that menace you — menace Red. Rock Ranch."

"I'm sorry," repeated the girl. "It's no use going on."

The lawyer's mouth tightened like a steel trap. "You won't get any help from Boicer." He spoke sneeringly. "All Boicer wants is your ranch. He doesn't love you. He's got a dozen women on the string."

"Aren't you a bit insulting?" Benita pushed up from her chair, her eyes bright with anger. "I wish you would go!"

"I'm not finished." Iswell drew a large envelope from the inside pocket of his linen coat. "Your refusal to consider my —" He saw that her attention was distracted by something behind him. He turned and looked. Fred Craler stood framed against the patio gate, shocked, eyes fixed on the rifle barrel that glinted in the bushes. A bridle and several leather latigos dangled from the crook of his arm.

Tomas moved toward him from the bushes. "What you want?" The Navajo's tone was curt.

"Hell — you know me, Tomas." Fred forced a sickly grin. "Got some stuff Tom Lucky had us order for him. I figgered he was in a hurry for it and fetched it out."

"Tom not here," the Indian told him. He lowered the carbine and held out a brown hand. "Me take —"

"Sure." Fred surrendered the merchandise, sent a sly look in the direction of Benita and Iswell. "Howdy, folks!"

"Stick around, Fred," Iswell called. "I'll ride you back to town in the buggy. You can put your horse on a lead-rope."

"Suits me," grinned the youth. "I don't crave to set a saddle when there's a soft buggy seat handy." He swung back to the gate.

154

Tomas watched him go, his expression uneasy. His look went uncertainly to Francisco who seemed to he drowsing in his chair. The old Mexican's hand tapped the long barrel of the shotgun across his knees, a motion that only the Navajo's sharp eyes saw. Rifle in lowered hand, Tomas went up the path to the *galeria*. He held up the bridle and latigos as he passed Benita and Iswell. "Me take to office," he said.

Benita merely nodded. She sensed the purpose that was taking Tomas to the office had nothing to do with the gear Fred had brought for Tom Lucky. The place for such things was in the saddle-room in the barn. She only half heard the lawyer's voice. She was trying to fathom what was in the Navajo's mind. Something to do with Fred Craler. She had noticed the Indian's momentary indecision as he watched the youth disappear through the gate. Larkin Iswell's words suddenly riveted her attention.

"I would have been willing to destroy this piece of paper," the lawyer was saying. "In fact it is not too late, Benita. It is up to you, my dear." He smoothed the folds from the sheet of paper he took from the envelope. "As the matter stands, it will be very difficult, if not impossible, for you to find one hundred thousand dollars — a considerable amount larger, with the interest."

"I — I don't understand!" Benita stared at him. The malicious triumph in his eyes chilled her.

"It's very simple," smiled the lawyer. "A business transaction between your father and me."

155

A feeling of impending disaster held her speechless. She could only continue to stare.

"I loaned your father the sum of one hundred thousand dollars," Iswell continued. "He needed the money in a great hurry and I was able to let him have it." Iswell gestured. "His own word would have been good enough, but naturally he insisted upon this note."

She found her voice. "Note? Why — why I can't believe it! My father was not a borrower — and he would never have gone to you!"

"You do me an injustice." The lawyer's tone was offended.

"It is incredible," Benita insisted. She was pale, more frightened than she cared to admit. Larkin Iswell would not dare to say Ben Ellison had borrowed the money unless he could prove the assertion. And it seemed that he could. She gazed dumbly at the sheet of paper in Iswell's hand.

"I am not a liar." He looked at her with cold, glassy eyes. "My reputation is not to be questioned. Ask anybody in Palo Pinto. Lending money is my business. I am what you call a private banker as well as a lawyer. I shall not allow you to slander me."

"Let me see it, please." She held out her hand.

"Certainly." Iswell put the note into her fingers. Benita read it carefully. It seemed to prove his claim. Her father had borrowed the sum of one hundred thousand dollars. The date went back more than two years. A demand note and no payments shown.

Her heart sank. Where could she find a hundred thousand dollars, a lot more than that, with the accrued interest? It was odd that her father had not even paid the interest.

Iswell was watching her with merciless eyes. "Yes," he said. "A lot of money, with all that interest. I was not worried. The money was safe enough and your father would have paid the note in good time." He smiled faintly. "It's up to you, now that he is dead."

Benita understood. Instinct told her that Larkin Iswell was going to demand immediate payment. He would take his revenge for her almost contemptuous rejection of his offer of marriage.

He smiled again, maliciously, as if reading her horrified thoughts. "I'm afraid I must press for immediate payment," he said. "I have waited long enough. Blame your father — not me."

She flashed him an outraged look, returned her attention to the note. It seemed all right to her inexperienced eyes, and yet — something seemed not quite right.

Benita went rigid and for a long moment she sat there, wide-eyed gaze fixed on the paper in her hands.

Iswell broke the silence. "I'm quite sure you see how useless it is to dispute my claim." He spoke with a certain uneasiness not lost on her.

Her head lifted in a long, steady look at him. The fear had gone from her eyes. She was smiling derisively. "Oh, but I *do* dispute it, Mr. Iswell." She spoke coolly.

His own composure wilted under the contempt in her eyes. "You can't!" he stammered. "It's a legal claim that will ruin you."

She thrust the note back at him. "It's quite worthless," she said quietly. "You won't dare to offer that thing in any court." She stood up, her eyes sparkling. "I think you will be wise to go — before Francisco starts killing his snake."

Iswell's head jerked around in a look. The old Mexican grinned, put the shotgun to his shoulder and squinted down the twin barrels. "*Si*," he rumbled. "I keel heem r-rattlesnik."

Iswell cowered behind a big stone pillar that supported the *galeria* roof. "I — I'm going," he babbled. "My God — do you want another murder here?"

At a look from the girl, Francisco lowered the shotgun. Iswell stuffed the note into its envelope, crammed the envelope back in his coat pocket and grabbed his hat and linen duster. "You will regret this," he said venomously.

Benita shook her head. "Abel Gregg was right about you," she said. "You are a mean little crook. As if my father would have anything to do with a scamp like you!" She was enjoying herself, reveling in his discomfiture. She had not felt so good for days. "Get out of here — and don't ever come back."

The staccato crash of guns in the ranch yard shocked her to silence. She forgot Larkin Iswell, ran as fast as her feet could move to the patio gate. The lawyer started to follow, came to an abrupt standstill under the threat of the shotgun old Francisco promptly leveled at him.

Benita pulled the gate open, stood there, looking in the direction of the barn. She saw the body of a man sprawled on the ground. She saw other things — the three hounds, huddled limp shapes near the watering trough — and she saw Fred. Craler, a smoking gun in his hand.

He caught sight of her, started in her-direction. "Miss Ellison!" His voice was a high-pitched scream. "Ringer Barran was layin' poison for the dogs! He's killed Tomas!"

The ground rocked under Benita's feet. She put out steadying hand to the gate. Behind her she heard the quick-padding feet of Raquel Perez.

"The Blessed Mary help us!" babbled the old woman in Spanish. "The black curse of death is on this place."

CHAPTER
FIFTEEN

Benita started running again. Toward the limp form sprawled on the ground. She was vaguely aware of a faint drumming sound — the hammering hoofs of fast-running horses. She was aware too, of something else — the face of Fred Craler, stamped with insensate lust to kill. His protruding upper teeth had the look of a snarling wolf. The truth struck her with a sickening impact that again brought her to a standstill. Instinctively her hand fastened over the gun in her belt.

Fred Craler raced up, dust spurting from bootheels. He had a long-legged, gangling stride that carried him with amazing speed. He slid to a halt, his breath coming in gulps that made his words unnaturally thin and jerky. "Barran was hand-feedin' poison to the dogs. Tomas come sneakin' from the barn. He wasn't fast enough and Barran killed him." Fred brushed back an unkempt lock of black hair. "I pulled my gun on Barran but he got clean away. He was ridin' that buckskin an' be sure burned up dust." The youth darted a furtive look at the gun in Benita's clenched hand. His too-small head seemed to weave from side to side, his tongue flicked over his thin lips. He was suddenly silent, staring at her with eyes that were like slits of glass. Benita thought of a snake, making ready to strike.

She managed to find her voice, was surprised at her coolness. "The sheriff is coming, Fred. Quick — run and tell him about Barran being here."

Craler's head jerked around. His expression changed. It was apparent he had not noticed the approaching riders. The gun in his hand vanished like magic inside his shirt. "I'll tell Clant which way he headed," he said. He began to run toward the big yard gate.

Benita was running too, toward the inert form lying there on the far side of the watering trough. She heard Fred Craler's high-pitched voice shouting words to the horsemen galloping into the yard. She made no attempt to look at the newcomers, could think only of Tomas.

She went down on her knees by his side. Her heart was pounding, she could hardly see through the tears that blurred her eyes. Her hand went out to touch him. She drew it back hastily with a sharp intake of her breath. The Navajo's eyes were open, looking up at her. Unutterable relief rushed through her. She started to speak, saw that he wanted her silence. He spoke with painful slowness, his words hardly audible. "*No say me not dead.*"

Benita's lips formed a single word. "*Why?*" She held her breath for his answer.

His only response was a feeble shake of his head. His eyes fluttered, closed.

Benita continued to kneel there, her gaze on him, her thoughts racing, delving for a reason that would explain his words. The answer came. Tomas wanted the man who shot him to believe him dead. If he thought Tomas would live to betray his identity the killer would try again — make an effort to finish the job.

She got to her feet. She must do all she could to keep the killer from knowing that Tomas was not dead. The Indian was evidently badly wounded. She had to work with desperate swiftness to keep him from dying on her hands.

Benita, was amazed at her own coolness at that moment. Plans were taking shape as she ran toward the group of riders who were listening to Fred Craler's excited account of the shooting. She was going so fast she almost tripped over one of the dead hounds. She was aware of blood, a gaping wound, but made no attempt to understand. Her one thought was to hide the fact that Tomas was not dead.

She paused briefly to speak to Raquel who was running from the patio gate to meet her. "Pretend to faint . . . be very ill," she said in Spanish. "Quick — do not question!"

Raquel promptly screamed, collapsed in the dust. Benita bent over her with a frightened cry. A shout came from Sheriff Boicer. He swung from his saddle and ran with short, choppy strides that lifted riffles of golden yellow dust. Two other men followed. One of them was Abel Gregg.

"Sure is one hell of a business," grumbled the sheriff. "Ringer Barran was here, Fred says. Killed the Injun and got clean away. I'm sure out of luck." He glowered down at the plump form of Raquel Perez; "She get a bullet, too?"

162

"It's shock," Benita told him. "Her heart." Her voice was tearful "We must send for Dr. Smeed at once."

"I'll have one of the boys go after him," offered Boicer. His tone was reluctant.

Benita shook her head. "Mr. Iswell is in the garden. He was just leaving. He can tell Dr. Smeed about poor Raquel." She looked at Abel Gregg.

Abel's penetrating, kindly eyes saw under the white mask of her face. He was puzzled, but quick to read the hidden appeal. "I'll get Lark," he said, and turned on his heel.

Sheriff Boicer showed signs of relief. His look went to the dead hounds, traveled on to the Indian's sprawled body. "Did you see the shootin', Benita?" he asked.

She shook her head. "I was in the garden — with Mr. Iswell —"

Boicer's eyes glinted jealously. "Saw Lark at the hotel this mornin'. He didn't say he was headin' this way." He shrugged dusty shoulders. "No sense wastin' time here. Fred says Barran ain't been gone only a few minutes. We'll get him if it means combin' every foot of chaparral within five miles. He ain't had time to get far." His gaze shifted to Tomas: "Maybe I should have a look at the Injun."

It was the last thing Benita wished him to do. Tomas wanted to be thought dead. She went down on her knees, took one of Raquel's hands in her own. "Oh, Clanton — she — she's hardly breathing. I'm frightened."

The use of his name pleased the sheriff. He forgot about the Indian, bent over Raquel for a closer look. "Sure looks bad," he muttered. He jerked a flask from a hip-pocket. "A shot of whiskey will maybe bring her 'round." He made a half-hearted attempt to force the fiery liquid into Raquel's month. Her teeth were tightly clenched and the whiskey trickled down her chin.

Boicer straightened up, returned the flask to his pocket. "I should be chasin' after Ringer Barran," he said fretfully.

"You needn't wait, Clanton," Benita urged. "You mustn't let him escape."

The repetition of his name brought a grin from the sheriff. "I'll get him," he assured her. "I reckon with Abel here you can handle things." He hesitated. "I'll be back this way. Got things I want to say." He gave her a meaning look as he turned away.

Benita bent more closely over Raquel whose left eye was opening in a aly look. "*Be careful!*" she hissed in a low whisper.

"What'd you say, Benita?" The sheriff halted, looked back at her.

"I said *hurry!* You won't catch him if you don't hurry."

The sheriff hastened his stride. "Let's ride, fellers!" he bawled. "That damn killer ain't had time to get far. I ain't restin' till we slap him back in jail."

Dust lifted and drifted across the yard as the posse rode away and disappeared in the chaparral beyond the barn. Abel Gregg and Larkin Iswell hurried from the patio gate. The lawyer made for his buggy. Abel

164

followed, snatched the tie-rope loose. Iswell scrambled into the seat, darted an ugly look at the girl bent over the Mexican woman. Fred Craler ran up with his horse on a lead-rope. He climbed into the buggy.

Abel's shaggy brows knotted in a frown. "You could make town a lot quicker on the horse, Fred," he said. "We want Doc Smeed soon as he can get here."

"I'm stickin' with Mr. Iswell," Fred answered sulkily. "I ain't takin' chances of runnin' into that killer by my lonesome."

Abel gave him a disgusted look, stood watching until the buggy disappeared around a bend in the avenue. Benita's urgent voice swung him toward her. Amazement widened his eyes. Raquel Perez was on her feet and running across the yard to the prostrate Indian, her voluminous skirt bunched high in one hand. It was obvious that Raquel was very far from being a sick woman.

Benita understood his surprise. "Abel — he's not dead!" She sped after Raquel.

Abel began running, too. He bent over the unconscious Indian, made a quick examination of the wound. His gaze lifted in a puzzled look at the girl.

"Tomas didn't want it known, he was not dead," Benita said. "Oh, Abel — it's dreadful! I can't stop to explain. We must get him to a safe place where we can nurse him."

Abel wasted no time with questions. "He's a heavy man —"

"We will help —" Benita broke off, beckoned the two Mexican girls watching from the patio gate. "Delfina — Pepa!" she called. "Come and help!"

Between them, they carried Tomas to a bedroom in the big house. Abel was no stranger to gunshot wounds. He went to work, assisted by the capable Raquel.

"Nothin' more we can do until the doc gets here," he finally said. "We've got the bleedin' stopped. It's up to the doc to dig that bullet out."

"He won't die?" Benita's voice was shaky.

"He's plenty tough," Abel replied. "I'd say that bullet wasn't wearin' his name." He stared at her curiously. "I'm some confused. Ain't got it straight why you didn't want Boicer and the fellers to know Tomas wasn't dead."

"I'm confused myself," Benita told him with a shiver. "You see — I'm not quite sure about what happened."

"This talk is not good for poor Tomas," scolded Raquel. She looked compassionately at the Navajo. "I will watch until the doctor comes," she added.

Abel followed the girl out to the cool shade of the *galeria*. "I'm sure puzzled," he complained. "Raquel ain't no more sick than I am."

Benita smiled into his perplexed eyes. "I couldn't say I wanted Dr. Smeed for Tomas. He was supposed to be dead. I had to think up some other reason — and Raquel was *it*. I *told* her to faint."

"You're a fast thinker," chuckled Abel. His keen eyes probed her. "You ain't answered my question," he went on soberly. "Why didn't you tell Boicer that Tomas wasn't dead?"

166

Benita hesitated. She was reminded of the sheriff's promise to return — his smirking announcement that he had things to say to her. The thought was dismaying. She saw that Abel was watching her curiously. "I had two reasons," she said. "Tomas didn't want me to tell anybody —"

"You told *me*," Abel interrupted dryly.

"I trust *you*."

"Meanin' you don't trust Clant Boicer?"

"That's the second reason," admitted Benita. "I don't know why, exactly, but I don't trust him. I think father didn't either," she added thoughtfully.

Abel nodded. "Ben was awful set 'gainst Clant bein' sheriff," he said. "I've a notion Ben had his reasons. He didn't like Clant any too well."

"He's coming back, tonight, he said." Benita's tone was disconsolate. "He's the sheriff — and there's been a murder here. I can't tell the sheriff to keep away from this ranch."

Abel scowled. "Like as not he'll run into Kenzie if we ain't careful. Wish we could hear from Oliphant. Kind of ties Rand's hands — havin' to keep on the dodge from Clant." He shook his head worriedly. "Mighty queer the way Clant sticks to the notion that Rand is Ringer Barran."

Benita was silent. She felt she knew of *one* reason that would explain the sheriff's determination to make a swift and sure end of Rand Kenzie.

Abel noticed the wave of color in her cheeks. He said mildly, "No call for us to get jumpy about Rand. He's too smart for Clant Boicer."

167

CHAPTER
SIXTEEN

Twilight's mantle lay on the canyon's rugged slopes. Rand stripped saddle and bridle from the buckskin and turned the horse loose. Mingo promptly nosed out a desirable spot and enjoyed a leisurely roll. He scrambled upright and turned inquiring eyes on Rand who shook his head regretfully. He'd be back later with a good feed of grain, he told the horse. Mingo made snorting noises, switching his fine black tail and fell to cropping the short yellowing grass.

Rand replaced the brush barricade across the narrow opening between the cliffs. He turned away, halted abruptly, every sense instantly alert. Something was not quite right.

It was difficult to see in those deepening shadows, yet he was acutely aware of a difference since he had ridden away that morning.

He stood there, puzzled, disturbed. There *was* a difference. Those insistent little danger signals were not to be ignored.

It was his nose that brought him an inkling of the truth. Horses, and horses indicated visitors, probably Sheriff Boicer and his deputies.

It was a disturbing solution. It proved that Boicer was uncomfortably hot on the trail. The sheriff could not have failed to read the signs correctly. He would guess that the man he sought had been using the little rock-walled enclosure as a hideout.

Another and more reassuring thought came to Rand. It was unlikely the sheriff would repeat his search immediately. The horse would be safe enough for the night, or for such time necessary to learn more of the sheriff's activities.

His mind somewhat eased, Rand went on his way through the swiftly closing darkness.

He was soon moving cautiously between the tamarisks that hedged the path to the ranch office. Lamplight glowed through the curtained window. Somebody inside was talking. Rand recognized the sheriff's strident voice. He came to a dismayed standstill.

"I ain't going to rush you, Benita," the sheriff was saying. "It's for your own good. You need a husband, a man who savvys cattle and can run the ranch right."

"I'm sorry —" The girl's voice was troubled, almost frightened. Rand resisted the impulse to open the door and step into the office.

The sheriff was speaking again, urging, roughly tender "Your dad was set on it. He was likin' the idea of havin' me for a son-in-law. He used to say the Rafter B and the Block R would hook up awful well."

There was no reply from Benita. The sheriff changed the subject to Ringer Barran. "Fred Craler was right about him being the feller that killed the Injun. We run

169

across his hideout, down in the canyon back of the barn."

"How do you know it was his hideout?" Benita's apparent indifference drew a grim smile from Rand.

"Plenty sign there for a smart man to read," the sheriff answered with a satisfied laugh. "That buckskin horse has done some rollin' — left bits of hair layin' 'round."

"He must be a long way from here by now," Benita said. "He's too clever for you," she added spitefully. "I don't think you'll ever catch him."

"You bet I'll get him." Boicer's tone was gruff. "Well, so long, Benita. I'm headin' with the boys over to Rafter B. We got to get a fresh string of broncs."

Rand heard the door close, the scrape and jingle of spurs. He continued to wait, motionless in the blackness of the tamarisks. The sheriff's footsteps faded down the garden. The patio gate slammed and soon other sounds drifted from the big yard — the thud of hoofs as the sheriff and his men rode on their way.

Rand guessed that Benita had been listening too. He heard her quick, light step, and she was suddenly pulling the door open, stood framed, against the lamplight. The sight of her made Rand's pulse quicken.

"I knew you were here," she said with a grave little smile. "I was terribly frightened."

He stepped inside. Benita closed the door and drew the concealing curtain. He said ruefully, "I must have been clumsy — for you to know I was outside."

She shook her head. "It wasn't any sound you made."

170

Something held them suddenly wordless. They could only look at each other. It was the girl who finally spoke, her voice not quite steady. "Sheriff Boicer was here. I was so afraid he would hear you."

"I heard *him!*" Rand said.

The savageness in his voice drew a fleeting smile from her, then soberly, "He has found that place where you keep your horse."

Rand grinned. "I saw sign there'd been visitors."

"A lot has happened here since you went away this morning." She broke off, went to the patio door and pulled it open. Abel Gregg stepped inside from the darkness of the *galeria*.

"Hello, son." He gave Rand a grim smile. "Been plenty hell goin' on here."

"Let's have it from the beginning," Rand suggested.

Benita gave him the details briefly. "Fred Craler said he saw a man riding away on a buckskin horse," she finished.

"The lying little skunk," grumbled Abel. He glowered at Rand. "As good as claims it was you that poisoned the hounds and shot Tomas."

"How many shots did you hear?" Rand asked the girl.

"Four. One was a rifle shot."

"That would be from the Injun's carbine," Abel surmised. "I took a look at that carbine of his. He'd fired one shot."

Rand asked another question. "You heard nobody ride away, Benita?"

She shook her head. "Nobody," she asserted. "I reached the gate in a few seconds and saw only Fred Crater, a smoking gun in his hand. He said he had taken a shot at Ringer Barran." She paused, added with a shudder, "He looked like a fiend. I thought he was going to kill me."

"What do you make of it, son?" Abel spoke in a hard voice. It was obvious the question was one he had already settled to his own satisfaction.

"Benita heard four shots," Rand said. "One was fired by Tomas. The killer fired three times, shot Tomas and the two hounds. He had only time enough to poison one of the hounds before Tomas jumped him. Craler lied about a man on a buckskin horse and taking a shot at him. You would have heard five shots, and you would have heard the horse running."

"That's the picture," agreed Abel. "Ain't no doubt about it, Rand. It was Fred Craler done that shootin'."

"It also proves he's the man who poisoned all the other hounds," Rand pointed out.

Benita's face was a study in bewilderment. "It's too hideous!" she exclaimed. "Why would Fred Craler want to poison the hounds?"

"Your father wrote there were things going on that troubled him," reminded Rand. "The dog poisoning began some time back — before old Tom Lucky was killed under the rock slide."

"Yes," Benita said. "It did —"

"The ground was being prepared for murder," Rand continued. "I think we are going to find out that old Tom Lucky was killed before the rock slide got him."

Abel shifted uneasily in his chair. "I've a notion that maybe Benita should get away from this ranch for a spell."

"You can forget it," Benita retorted. "I'm not going to be frightened away from my own home."

Abel wagged his head dubiously. "Won't be your home for long — if Lark Iswell figgers to collect that note."

"I'm not worried about that note." The scorn in her voice drew keen looks from the two men. "It's bogus," she told them. "I can prove it."

"You seem very certain," Rand commented.

"I read the note carefully," Benita continued. "Only one thing wrong with it —" She smiled faintly. "Father didn't put his name to it."

"You said you saw his signature," Rand objected.

"The signature was perfect as far as it went," smiled the girl. "It happens that father used a special signature for important papers concerning the ranch. That is why I know the signature on Iswell's note is a forgery."

Abel Gregg straightened up in his chair, stared shrewdly at her. "I reckon I'm beginnin' to savvy," he said in a relieved voice. "You mean that note was signed *Ben Ellison*, huh?"

"That's right," she confirmed.

"The doggone crook," muttered Abel. "You bet I savvy. Ben always signed legal papers about ranch business some different from the way he'd sign a letter. His legal signature was *Benjamin Ellison y Ibarra*, which proves he never signed that note Iswell figgers to collect a hundred thousand dollars on."

"Which means Iswell fell into a trap," chuckled Rand.

Benita nodded. "*Rancho Piedra Rosa* is an old Spanish grant," she explained. "Mother was the last Ibarra and the actual owner, which was why father always followed the old custom of combining their names on legal papers. He liked it that way." She went to the desk, opened a drawer and extracted a large document. "This will show you father's legal signature, or *rubrica*, as it was called in the old days before the gringo."

Rand studied the intricate flourishes of loops, circles and zigzag lines that was Ben Ellison's legal signature. It was not a thing to be duplicated except by the originator of its mysteries.

"You see what I mean?" Benita replaced the document in the drawer.

"Yes," Rand answered soberly. "I see a lot of things. I see Larkin Iswell — and he doesn't look good in this business."

"Listen —" Abel's frown indicated he was straining his memory. "Ben was wantin' some quick cash. Hadn't time to send to Las Cruces and got Lark Iswell to lend him a thousand. It all comes back to me. I'd have fixed him up myself only I didn't have a thousand handy that day. Ben got it from Lark. He wasn't likin' the notion. Ben never had no use for Lark."

"When was this?" inquired Rand.

174

"Wasn't long before the time Ben was shot," Abel replied. "It all comes back to me. Ben give Iswell his note for the loan. I saw it." Abel smiled dryly. "I reckon Ben didn't think it was important enough for him to put in time workin' out his *rubrica*. He just put his own Ben Ellison to the thing."

"Explains a lot," commented Rand. "Ben didn't know it, but he set a trap that Iswell fell into."

"I ain't finished," continued Abel. "Ben was in town a day or two later and he paid Iswell that thousand in cash. I was with him when we run into Iswell in the hotel lobby. Ben hauled a roll of bills from his pocket and counted out the money in front of me. Iswell said the note was in his office. Ben was in a rush to head back to the ranch and he told Iswell he'd drop in for the note next time he was in town." Abel paused, shook his head sorrowfully. "Ben never did get to town ag'in."

There was a long silence. They knew what Abel meant. Rand fought off an impulse to go to the white-faced girl — take her in his arms. She seemed to feel the impact of his look. Her dark head went up defiantly. "I'm past crying about it." She spoke almost fiercely. "It's time for fighting — not crying."

"That's talk your dad would like," Abel Gregg said gruffly. He got out of his chair, patted her shoulder. "You ain't fightin' this thing alone. Not while I can lift a gun."

Rand sat motionless in his chair, his thoughts racing, picking up and discarding the pieces, slowly fitting the right ones in their proper places. Abel's next words held him rigidly attentive.

"Doc Smeed figgers old Sundown was out of his head when he said it."

"Said what?" Rand asked sharply.

"Why — accordin' to the doc, Sundown claims it was Tony Silver shot him up in Piñon Pass."

"That's absurd!" exclaimed Benita. "Sundown must have been delirious."

"That's Doc Smeed's notion," agreed Abel. He met Rand's intent gaze. "I take it you ain't so sure the doc's right, huh?" His tone was suddenly grim.

"There are a lot of loose pieces lying around," Rand replied. He gave the old man a searching look. "You have something on your mind, Abel."

"Well —" Abel's tone was cautious. "I kind of figgered the same way as the doc about Sundown . . . figgered he was ravin' plenty. Wasn't till I got to chawin' it over in my mind that I remembered somethin' about Tony Silver."

Benita widened her eyes in a startled look. "Abel —" She spoke excitedly. "You mean about our seeing Tony Silver riding out of the arroyo just as we left Dr. Smeed's house?"

"You're smart — awful smart." Abel nodded his head approvingly. "We figgered Tony had been huntin' quail down in the wash. Maybe we was wrong. Maybe Tony *had* been gettin' him a bag of quail. He could maybe have been as far as Piñon Pass." He gestured hopelessly. "There you are, son. Some more of them loose pieces to wrastle with."

"Too many pieces." Rand grimaced. "I've turned up some pieces my own self." He gave them a brief account of his visit to Lobo Mesa.

Abel Gregg wagged his head sorrowfully. "I ain't so awful surprised about Tom Lucky," he commented. "He's an ongrateful pup."

"It's terrible." Benita was visibly shocked. "It's hard to believe —" She broke off, stared with dismayed eyes at Rand. "What *shall* we do?"

"Ace Bruff and Slim Purdy should be here soon," Rand said.

"Ace and Slim make a pair to draw to," Abel observed. "Tom was a fool to think them two would fall for his low-down play."

"Only one thing we can do with Tom when he gets here," Rand continued. "We'll make it impossible for him to meet Barran at Burnt Wagon Springs tomorrow night."

"He's sure due for a surprise," muttered Abel. He looked speculatively at Rand. "You've proved one thing, son. Clant Boicer was right about the feller that shot Ben was ridin' a buckskin. And Lark Iswell was right about the feller bein' Ringer Barran, although it's mighty queer Lark claims *you* are Barran. He sure knows different, even if Clant don't. Clant only knows the feller was ridin' a buckskin. That was enough for him to want you in jail."

Rand's eyes narrowed thoughtfully. "I'm not so sure it was Ringer Barran who shot Ben," he said. "Are *you* sure, Abel?"

Abel was suddenly wary. His head lifted in a sharp look. "I figger it's a good guess," he replied cautiously.

"Of course it was Ringer Barran," Benita asserted. "I think that is a strange question. Rand."

Rand was silent for a moment. "I had a close look at Barran," he finally said. "He carried a rifle in his saddle boot, and wore two guns." Rand paused, added significantly, "I didn't notice that he carried a shotgun."

Benita was plainly bewildered. "I don't understand," she began. Abel interrupted her. "You're smart, son." He spoke with an excitement unusual in him.

The girl's perplexed look went from one to the other. Rand said quietly, "You see, Benita, the man who killed your father used a *shotgun*."

"Oh!" She frowned, shook her head. "If — if it was not Barran — who else?" She gestured despairingly. "It makes it all the more mysterious — difficult."

"We know it wasn't Barran who shot Tomas," ruminated Abel.

"You mean it might have been Fred Craler who shot father?" Benita's tone was dubious. "We are doing a lot of guessing. We can't know for certain about Fred Craler until Tomas is able to tell us just what did happen in the yard."

"I'll stick to the guessin'," drawled the old frontiersman. "It's my guess it was Fred who poisoned the hounds from the start and it's my guess he shot the Injun." Abel's tone was triumphant. "Addin' up the guesses makes a total that reads Fred Craler."

"We really don't know about Fred," persisted the girl. "We can't know until Tomas is able to tell us."

"What's *your* notion about it, son?" Abel challenged. "Any ideas?"

Rand shook his head. "We're still in the guessing stage," he answered dryly. "I may be wrong about Barran. The chances are I'm not wrong. He's mixed up in it, though, and it's probable he knows the truth about the supposed accident that killed old Tom Lucky."

"It gets worse and worse," Benita said despondently. "It's too confusing."

Dr. Smeed pushed into the office. He dropped his bag on a chair and drew a pipe from a bulging coat pocket. "Well, well," he said, staring hard at Rand. "If I'm not mistaken you are the man Sheriff Boicer had in jail on a murder charge."

"Listen!" Benita was indignant. "Mr. Kenzie is a friend of mine. Don't be silly, Doctor."

Dr. Smeed tamped a charge of tobacco into the charred bowl of his pipe. "I've been too busy to keep up with the news," he complained. "So Mr. Kenzie is Mr. Kenzie — and not the notorious Ringer Barran?" He chuckled. "I must tell Boicer he is a fool."

"You mustn't!" exclaimed Benita. "We don't want Sheriff Boicer to know Mr. Kenzie is here."

"That's right, Doc," Abel said with a shake of his head. "We've got good reasons for not wantin' Clant to know about Rand. He's been nosin' 'round here a lot today at that."

"All right, all right." The doctor gave Rand a genial smile. "Your word is good enough for me, Abel."

"How is Tomas makin' out?" Abel inquired.

"He'll pull through," prophesied the doctor. He puffed hard on the pipe, fished something from his waistcoat pocket. "Here's the bullet."

Abel examined the flattened piece of lead curiously, then flipped it across to Rand. "Come out of a derringer," he said laconically.

Rand pocketed the bullet without comment. The doctor said casually, "Boicer claims Barran shot Tomas. Is that right?"

Abel grinned. "The piece of lead you just give me don't back up the sheriff's claim. A gent like Ringer Barran wouldn't pack a gun small enough for that bullet."

Dr. Smeed gestured with his pipe. "You should know, Abel." He paused, a curious expression in his eyes. "It was a lot bigger bullet that smashed through Sundown Skaggs, and that reminds me of something queer the old fellow said this morning."

"You mean his talk about Tony Silver?" drawled Abel. "Has Sundown talked some more?"

"He was raving, of course," declared the doctor. "No, he's too sick to do any coherent talking."

Rand was watching the doctor uneasily. "Have you mentioned it to anyone else?" he asked abruptly.

The question seemed to annoy the doctor. He frowned, answered testily. "Is it important?"

"Very." The hard note in Rand's voice made Dr. Smeed stare.

180

"Well —" The physician pondered, "I may have mentioned it. The thing seemed so ridiculous."

"Anybody in particular?" Rand put the question in the same hard voice.

Something like worry appeared in the doctor's eyes. He hesitated. "I mentioned it to Tony Silver. He had a good laugh. That big belly of his fairly shook."

The ensuing silence deepened the frown on the doctor's ruddy face. "What's wrong?" he fretted.

"That's a question," Abel Gregg answered in his quiet voice. "We ain't knowin' for certain there's anythin' wrong."

"I'm not a fool," snapped Dr. Smeed: "You mean I shouldn't have told Tony Silver?"

"That's about it," Abel answered dryly. "There's things we know that *you* don't. At that we're kind of guessin' wild."

"I'm stumped," complained Dr. Smeed. He puffed furiously on his pipe.

Rand got up from his chair. He said curtly, "I'm riding —"

Benita divined his purpose. She sprang to her feet. "No!" she exclaimed. "You mustn't!"

He disregarded her protest. "You stay here with Benita," he said to Abel. "It's up to you to handle Tom Lucky when he gets in. Ace and Slim may show up before Tom comes."

"I savvy," Abel said.

"Tom mustn't get away," Rand warned.

"He won't," promised Abel. A hard smile wrinkled his leathery face. "Not from Ace Bruff he won't."

181

Rand's look went briefly to the girl. "Don't worry." A hint of a smile warmed his eyes. She ran to him, but this time no protest came from her. "You are right — and good luck, Rand."

His look thanked her and the next instant he was gone through the little side door. The bewildered doctor stared at Abel and Benita.

"What is taking him off in such a confounded hurry?"

"Well — it's like this. Doc —" Abel spoke without his customary drawl. "Rand figgers there's folks in town that will want to shut Sundown's mouth for keeps."

Dr. Smeed's pleasant face lost some of its ruddiness. "*My God!*" He gave them an aghast look and turned quickly to the patio door. "I'm getting back to Palo Pinto as fast as that team of mine can run." The door slammed behind him and they heard the quick beat of his feet fade down the walk.

They heard other sounds — the thud of hoofs in the yard.

"I reckon that will be Ace and Slim gettin' in," Abel said in a relieved voice.

Benita only nodded. Her thoughts were with Rand Kenzie, somewhere out in the dark night. She might never again see him, for she knew now with terrible certainty that death indeed stalked the range.

CHAPTER
SEVENTEEN

There were times when memories held sleep at bay from Pablo Casado. He would lie on the straw mattress, ears unconsciously absorbing the sounds that drifted in from the night. It was often this way with him when the moon was down and the stars behind blanketing clouds. His thoughts would reach back through the years to the turbulent days of his lusty youth when he rode with the revolutionists below the border. Always the dark hours were the perilous hours when a man would awaken from the sleep of exhaustion only to plunge into eternity under the death thrust of an enemy *machete*.

Pablo fingered the great scar on his cheek, muttered a malediction. He was a fool to lie awake. A man must have his sleep or he was good for nothing.

The sound of voices in the corral jerked him upright. He listened for a moment, fingers curled over the handle of the *machete* that never left his side. Manuel Vargas! Why would Manuel be in the corral so close to midnight?

The Mexican slid from his straw mattress, hitched the leather belt around his paunchy middle and went on soundless feet from the little room at the far end of the barn.

He found Vargas repairing a brake block on one of his huge wagons. His swamper stood watching with sleepy, resentful eyes, a lantern dangling from his hand.

"You work too late, or too early," complained Pablo.

The freighter gave him a gloomy look. "There is good reason," he said. "It is time for haste. I must be on my way before I am caught like a lamb in the jaws of a wolf." He wiped his hot face with the back of his hand and stared morosely at the broken brake block.

"You talk riddles," grumbled Pablo. "Who is this wolf from whom you run?"

"It is by chance that I heard the news," Manuel told him. "This Señor Bleeker is a sleek scheming devil — a liar beyond all liars."

"It is the truth," agreed Pablo. "A rascal, which is no news to me."

"He is a cheat," Manuel Vargas said bitterly. "I brought in much goods for him, five tons, and he would pay me for only four tons." The freighter spat contemptuously. "We have the big row . . . much talk and I tell him that no more will I come with my wagons to Palo Pinto. He does not like my talk and tonight I get the news from a good friend that this gringo pig plans to swear out the warrant to arrest me."

"*Por Dios!*" exclaimed the shocked Pablo.

"It is so," affirmed Manuel wrathfully. "He waits to tell your sheriff that I have delivered boxes filled with gravel instead of the goods for which he paid his money."

184

"That is bad," sympathized Pablo. "You do well to run, my friend. Your word will not go far against the vile charge of this miserable storekeeper."

"I leave the moment this cursed brake block permits." Manuel's look went to the swamper. "Make haste, Chato . . . get the harness on the mules."

The swamper set the lantern on an up-ended box and broke into a run toward the barn. Manuel lighted a thin brown cigarette, stared worriedly at his friend. "This Bleeker pig sits up late tonight. I have kept an eye on his store and a light still burns in his office."

"I will watch for you," offered Pablo. "It is possible he suspects your purpose and has sent word to the sheriff."

He left the freighter tinkering with the defective brake and melted into the darkness. For all his bulk, the old Mexican could move with the stealth of a cat.

The swing lamp in front of Silver's Palace Bar was the only spot of light in the street. Several horses drooped at the hitch-rail in front of the saloon from which came intermittent bursts of drunken merriment.

Pablo halted, gaze on the dark front of Sam Bleeker's store. He could reassure Manuel Vargas the light no longer burned in the office. The storekeeper had evidently retired for the night.

Footsteps inside the building revived Pablo's interest, held him motionless, eyes glued on the two vague shapes that appeared in the doorway. A key clicked in the lock and the shapes moved across the street toward the saloon.

Unaware of the watching Mexican, the two men paused in the glare of the big kerosene lamp. Pablo recognized Sam Bleeker and Fred Craler. He saw Fred peer inside the swing doors, and suddenly the pair were vague shapes again, moving past him, past the dark front of Larkin Iswell's office and on around the corner.

Pablo let out a relieved breath. They were so close he could have touched them. He felt a contempt for these gringos who could be so unaware of his nearness. He was conscious, too, of a disturbing uneasiness.

He was too experienced a campaigner to ignore the little things that warned of danger. And he had promised Rand Kenzie to keep alert his eyes — his ears. He was curious to know the purpose that had taken Sam Bleeker and his clerk around to the back of Iswell's office. He stealthily followed, heard the back door open and close, heard the low murmur of voices.

Lamplight glowed faintly from a small side window. Pablo edged in close, put an eye to a small crack between the shade and the sill. It was a warm night and the window was open.

Larkin Iswell was sprawled in a leather arm chair, a bottle of whiskey on the table between him and Tony Silver. The lawyer was in his shirt sleeves. He looked worried and his thin, nasal voice lacked its customary smoothness. "We've got to think fast," he was saying to Sam Bleeker. "We've got to work fast."

The storekeeper lowered his lanky frame into a chair and poured himself a drink from the bottle. He lifted the glass, stared at Iswell, then at Tony Silver. The saloon man spread out his hands. "Lark spik gooda sense by damn yes."

Sam Bleeker seemed perturbed. He lowered the glass of whiskey to the table, pushed it toward his clerk. "You take it, Fred," he said.

"Chicken-hearted, that's what *you* are," sneered Iswell.

"I've always got along with Sundown." The storekeeper spoke sullenly. "I wish to God I hadn't listened to your talk, Lark. I've been making good in this town. This business is getting me scared."

"Leesen, you —" Tony Silver rapped the table with pudgy fingers. "I no like theesa talk from you by damn."

"Don't worry." Sam Bleeker reached for the bottle and filled another glass. "I'm in too deep to back out." He drained the glass, slammed it on the table and stared fixedly at his clerk. "It's my guess that Lark and Silver have a job for you, Fred."

"Tonight," Larkin Iswell said softly.

"Suits me," Fred Craler replied. His vicious grin slid over their intent faces. "Any time you say."

"It's got to be done right — and no comebacks," warned the lawyer.

"Leave it to me," grinned Craler. He reached for the bottle.

Pablo stealthily withdrew from the window. His prolonged absence would be causing Manuel Vargas much uneasiness. He went swiftly down the alley and after a cautious look, proceeded to the livery barn.

The Mexican was worried by what he had seen and overheard. The veiled reference to Sundown Skaggs puzzled him. Something was in the wind, and Fred Craler was involved. The thing mystified Pablo. He was a liberal subscriber to Palo Pinto's unflattering opinion of Sam Bleeker's clerk.

He found Manuel Vargas removing the bells from the lead team of the ten mule hitch now strung out in front of the wagons. He told the freighter of Sam Bleeker's whereabouts. "His mind is on other matters," Pablo said. "He does not suspect that you make the get-away."

"I will go quietly," Manuel said with a satisfied chuckle. "See — I take the bells from my little pets. There will be no music."

"That is wise," approved Pablo. "The Good God ride with you and your wagons, my friend. Dawn will find you many miles from this nest of snakes. You can then snap your fingers at the thrice accursed Bleeker."

"You are a good friend," rejoined the freighter. "We will meet again and I shall buy you many drinks."

"The day cannot come too soon," Pablo assured him courteously. He vanished into the black maw of the barn. A faint rustle of straw caught his alert ears, held him motionless, fingers curled hard on the haft of his *machete*.

A tall shape appeared from the end stall. Surprise widened the Mexican's eyes. "Señor," he whispered hoarsely.

"I'm in a rush," Rand said. "I want to get Sundown Skaggs away from the doctor's house. Have you a light wagon that will hold a cot?"

188

"*Por Dios*," muttered Pablo. "This is strange — what you say about Sundown."

The excitement in his voice held Rand rigid, drew his sharp look. "What do you mean?"

Pablo gave him a brief account of what he had seen and overheard. "It does not make sense," he grumbled.

"It means we must get Sundown away before Fred Craler kills him," Rand said grimly. "It's like this, Pablo, they want to shut Sundown's mouth because he claims it was Tony Silver who shot him up in Piñon Pass."

Pablo was incredulous. Not that he put murder past the always genial saloon man. *Por Dios!* He had seen the evil look on Tony Silver's face when he threatened Sam Bleeker. Tony was a bad one, but Pablo could not imagine Fred Craler killing anything more dangerous than a fly. Sounds drifted in from the night. The stamp of hoofs, the creak of heavy wheels. Pablo came out of his momentary daze. With a muttered exclamation be made for a side door, vanished into the darkness.

Rand jerked his gun from holster and cautiously followed. He saw the high shapes of the wagons, the strung-out mules, and Pablo in low-voiced conversation with the teamster. He hurried his stride, instantly aware of the purpose in Pablo's mind.

The Mexican gave him a grin as he joined them. "Manuel Vargas is a good friend," he reassured. He gestured at the ponderous canvas-covered wagons. "He agrees to the favor I ask."

"*Si*," grunted the freighter from his saddle. "Sundown is my friend a long time. I would not desert him to these dogs who seek his life."

CHAPTER
EIGHTEEN

Mrs. Simmons sat up in the bed with a start. Somebody was whispering her name. Or had she been dreaming?

The whispering continued, louder, more insistent. Mrs. Simmons reached for her flannel dressing gown and drew it over her shoulders. She called out in a low brisk voice, "Who is it?"

"Thees Pablo Casado, Señora," came the voice from the open window. "Queek, Señora. We 'ave come for take Sundown."

Mrs. Simmons pushed bare feet into slippers and hurried to the window. A second voice greeted her. "This is Rand Kenzie, Mrs. Simmons."

"Sure, I remember you. Wasn't you savin' Benita Ellison's life only yesterday?" Mrs. Simmons' voice was suddenly doubtful. "What's this talk of taking old Sundown away?" She peered with puzzled eyes at the two vague shapes outside.

Rand saw it was necessary to gain her confidence. He resorted to a half truth. "Dr. Smeed sent me," he told her. "We've got to get Sundown away to a safer place, Mrs. Simmons. There's a plot to kill him."

"You don't say!" The woman was aghast, and then, suspiciously, "And can you tell me where it was you saw doctor?"

"At the Ellison ranch," he answered. "Don't stop to argue about it."

Mrs. Simmons considered a moment. She was impressed by the authority in his voice. "I've seen you only the once," she said. "I says to Benita at the time you wall a man a woman could trust to kingdom come and I'll be eating me own words if I go to thinking different now. You'll find the front door unlocked," she added as she turned away.

She met them at the door, a small lamp in her hand. They followed her down the hall to a small room. Rand's look went to the patient.

"Is he awake?" he asked.

"He'll not waken for hours," Mrs. Simmons assured him. "He was that restless I gave him a sleeping powder."

Rand studied the wounded stage driver. "We'll take him mattress and all," he decided.

"He'll carry light," Mrs. Simmons said. "He's awful skinny." She hesitated. "You'll be wantin' me to come along with him?"

"We'll manage." Rand looked at the lamp in her hand. "Blow that light out."

She obeyed. The two men picked up the mattress and its occupant and started from the room.

Mrs. Simmons followed them to the porch. "Handle the poor man easy," she warned.

"Don't worry," Rand said. He hesitated. "Go back to your own house, Mrs. Simmons."

She sensed his anxiety. "This very minute. I'll not wait to put on me dress."

She watched for a few moments, bursting with curiosity, and marveling at their soundless disappearance into the covering blanket of the night. She was aware too of a sudden let-down, a trembling in her legs. The thing had happened so quickly. Less than five minutes had passed since those tapping fingers had awakened her, and now Sundown Skaggs was gone and she was alone — and decidedly frightened.

Mrs. Simmons wasted no more time with wild conjectures. She hastily pulled the doctor's door shut and hurried into the street. Her fright was quickened by the distant muffled beat of horses' hoofs. She decided it was no time to linger. Home sweet home was the proper place for her.

Rand and Pablo were half way across the belt of chaparral between the arroyo and the wagon road when they heard the horsemen.

"Boicer!" ejaculated Pablo in a disgusted voice. "The devil take that hombre!"

The situation worried Rand. If Pablo was right, the sheriff and his posse were too close for comfort.

"Manuel won't wait too long," he said. "We've got to hurry, Pablo."

They pushed on swiftly through the tangle of bushes and gently eased the wounded man's improvised stretcher under the covering branches of a greasewood close to the road.

Rand took a cautious look, saw with relief the high dark shapes of Manuel's big wagons. A tiny red glow in the blackness told him Manuel was waiting by the side of his wheel team.

The freighter dropped his cigarette, smothered a lingering spark with the toe of his boot. "Somebody comes," he said uneasily as Rand slid into view.

"The sheriff," Rand told him. "He must not find your wagons standing here. He'll be suspicious."

"*Si.*" Manuel swung a leg over the big wheel horse. "This is bad luck."

"Get the wagons moving, but don't go too far."

"I will wait beyond the bend," the freighter promised.

There was no time for more talk. The riders were already coming on around the bend, vague moving shapes drifting out of the black-walled night. Manuel spoke low words to his mules and the wagons went rumbling down the road.

From where he lay behind a sprawling greasewood Rand saw the moving shapes converge, heard the sheriff's loud voice. The wagons stopped their forward motion and for a moment no sound broke the night's stillness. Rand surmised that Boicer was sizing up the situation.

The sheriff spoke again, mingled surprise and suspicion in his voice. "Hell — it's *you*. What's the notion, Vargas? How come you're pullin' out so late?"

Manuel's somewhat halting explanation about much freight waiting in Socorro seemed only to increase the sheriff's suspicions.

"Are you sure you ain't got some stuff in your wagons you hadn't ought to have got?" he asked harshly. "Looks kind of queer, you pullin' out of town in the middle of the night."

Manuel was annoyed. His indignant protests left the sheriff unmoved.

"We'll take a look inside them wagons," he said. "Mind your manners, Vargas. I savvy Mex talk. I've a notion to slap you in jail for insultin' the law."

The search was quickly made. Rand heard the clatter of feet, the scrape of heavy tarpaulins.

"Nothin' in the wagons but what he's a right to have, Clant," reported a voice.

"All right, Vargas." The sheriff's disappointment was reflected in his, voice. "Wasn't knowin' but what you had some hombre hid away."

"*Por Dios*," fumed the freighter. "Thees loco joke you bet." He flung curt words at the mules and the wagons moved slowly away.

Rand held his breath as the posse streamed past. He was conscious of a vast satisfaction. The chance encounter with the sheriff had its good points. It was not likely he would search the wagons a second time. Not even to please Sam Bleeker if the storekeeper carried out his threat to charge Vargas with theft. The sheriff would be able to assure Bleeker that he had already searched the freighter's wagons.

Manuel's face were a contented grin when his friends hurried around the bend with the wounded Sundown on the makeshift stretcher. He also regarded the encounter as a blessing in disguise.

In a few moments the ponderous wagons were again rumbling along behind the fast-stepping mules. And sitting on his blanket roll in the rear wagon, Manuel's swamper gravely watched over Sundown Skaggs still sleeping soundly on his mattress.

Manuel Vargas had not lied to the sheriff. He actually was bound for the town of Socorro, with a little detour thrown in, a jog that would bring his wagons close to the Ellison ranch house. A profitable side-trip for the Mexican freighter, as evidenced by the twenty dollar gold piece that made pleasant music with other coins in his pocket.

Rand was aware of some misgivings as he watched the wagons vanish into the night. It was tough for old Sundown. Not what the doctor would order for a man suffering from a gunshot wound.

Pablo sensed his doubts, said shrewdly, "It is better the wagon than a knife in his heart."

Voices reached them from the street as they went silently back to the house. Pablo was worried. The sheriff was in town, he reminded Rand. "It will get your ears yet," grumbled the Mexican. "It is two dangerous — this thing you plan."

"It's worth a good try," Rand said curtly. He considered a moment. "I'm leaving it to you to have the horses ready."

"*Si.*" Pablo fingered his scarred cheek. "I would ride with you," he added wistfully. "It is like the old days."

Rand shook his head. "You must not be away from the barn if they come asking questions."

"That is true." Pablo nodded grimly. "I will tell them I see nothing, hear nothing and know nothing." He laughed softly, drifted like a shadow into the yawning blackness of the arroyo.

Rand worked his way stealthily around the doctor's small barn and finally reached the house. He managed to get a glimpse of the front door. It was closed, a fact he found reassuring. The man he was expecting would not have troubled to close the door if he had already made his sinister visit and discovered the disappearance of his intended victim. He would have suspected a trap and fled like a frightened rabbit.

Sounds of revelry drifted up the street from the saloon. Business had picked up since the arrival of the sheriff's posse. Rand's lips set in a hard grimace as he thought of Boicer. The sheriff would have learned the truth about Bert Ketcher by now. He had told Benita he was headed for his own Rafter B to get fresh horses. It must have been the shock of his life to find his foot-sore deputy safe, if not sound. Ketcher's story would add fuel to the sheriff's flaming hate of the man who was causing him so much misery.

Something was moving near the front steps, a soundless skulking shape. Rand tensed, fingers wrapped hard on the butt of his gun. The shape drew closer, went stealthily up the steps, paused for a moment then gently eased the door open and vanished inside the house.

Rand moved swiftly, crouched against the wall, close to the door. He waited, listening, gun in hand.

For a long moment no sound came from the darkness inside the house, then he heard the sputter of a match, the whisper of furtive feet as the intruder went hastily from room to room. The footsteps approached the door hurriedly, a quick slither of sound that told of rising panic.

The mysterious prowler was now in headlong flight. He came through the door with a rush, recoiled with a frightened animal-like whimper as he felt the hard press of Rand's gun.

"No noise, Craler," warned Rand. He jabbed his gun menacingly against the cringing spine.

"Who — who the hell are you?" Craler was breathing hard. He made no attempt to use the derringer clutched in his hand.

"I'm a rat-catcher," Rand said grimly. He jerked the little gun from his prisoner's grasp. The feel of it made him recall the piece of lead Dr. Smeed had extracted from the side of the wounded Indian. He pocketed the weapon and ordered Craler to face the wall.

The youth obeyed. He was shaking like a leaf. Rand pulled his hands behind his back and swiftly tied them with a short piece of cord. He snatched the handkerchief he saw in Craler's hip-pocket and fashioned a makeshift gag.

"All right," he said. "Let's go."

Craler was completely terrified. His knees sagged as Rand pushed him down the steps and on past the house toward the arroyo.

Pablo was waiting with the horses in the arroyo trail behind the livery barn. He shook his head regretfully as he helped Rand rope the prisoner to his saddle.

"It used to be we made quick work of such scum," he said in Spanish.

"He's more useful alive," Rand reminded. "He can tell us a lot of things we want to know. He is a good catch, Pablo."

"That is true," agreed the Mexican. He added solemnly, "You are a smart man. I would not want to be the one you hunted." His hand lifted in a parting gesture that also was a salute.

CHAPTER
NINETEEN

Loud voices awakened Pablo. He was not surprised to recognize the strident tones of Sheriff Boicer. It was very evident that the law officer was in a vile mood. Pablo pulled on his boots and cloaking his apprehensions with an ingratiating smile made his way to the men grouped in the pale dawn near the wide entrance. The night man threw him an appealing look, gestured helplessly.

Pablo gave the sheriff the benefit of his disarming smile. "W'at ees thees tr-rouble?" he asked mildly. "Who br-reak jail thees time?"

Boicer broke off his tirade, regarded the Mexican suspiciously. "Tryin' to be funny?" His tone was ominous.

Somebody guffawed. The sheriff whirled on the offender. "That's enough from you, Keno."

Keno grinned. "My gawd, Clant — cain't you take a joke?"

Boicer reddened, returned his attention to the two Mexicans. "No, Pablo — nobody has broke jail — but there *has* been a kidnapin' and if you fellers don't spill what you know about it I'll throw you in jail and keep you there till you rot."

"*Por Dios!*" exclaimed Pablo. "I no keednap nobody, señor. You make beeg joke wit' me."

"Yeah," sneered the sheriff, "a fine joke, but not on me, Pablo."

The old Mexican lifted an expressive shoulder, put out a protesting palm. Keno, delicately picking his teeth with a piece of straw, shook his head dubiously. "The Mex don't know nothin', Clant."

Boicer ignored him, fixed Pablo with angry, protuberant eyes. "Some feller made off with old Sundown," he said. "Sundown was too sick to walk out of town on his own legs, and you ain't makin' me believe he sprouted wings."

Pablo looked properly amazed. It was the work of the Evil One, he solemnly asserted.

"Yeah," again sneered Boicer. "Meanin' Ringer Barran, and I'm sure sendin' him back to jail where he belongs." The sheriff waggled a finger at the Mexican. "Barran was here last night. Ain't that right, Pablo?"

"I no savvy thees Ringer Barran," the Mexican answered truthfully. "*Por Dios!* You make beeg fool of me wit' thees loco talk."

A commotion outside the barn distracted the sheriff's attention. He glared impatiently at the cause of the disturbance. "Hell's fire, Sam! What's got *you* on the prod?"

"It's Fred!" gasped the storekeeper. "He ain't showed up!"

His agitation seemed oddly out of proportion to the news of his clerk's delinquency. Sheriff Boicer said as much in crisp words. "I'm the sheriff of this county," he heatedly reminded Sam Bleeker. "I ain't a nurse."

"Listen," pleaded the storekeeper. "Fred ain't at home — he ain't no place in town. He's clean gone from here."

The sheriff's jaw sagged as the import of Bleeker's words drove home. His gaze wandered stupidly from face to face, fastened on two men hurrying up from the street. Larkin Iswell and Tony Silver, both of them obviously quite as worried as Sam Bleeker.

Sheriff Boicer addressed them hoarsely. "What's on *your* minds? Who's missin' now from this damn cowtown?"

"It's serious business, Clant." Iswell spoke in a nervous, jerky voice, his suavity strangely lacking. "Why don't you get busy? These men must be found at once. It's up to you."

"Sure t'ing!" Tony Silver flapped his hands excitedly. "You find Sundown queek — or maybe more pipples get keel damn soon you bet!"

Sam Bleeker nodded solemnly. "That's right, Clant. I'm mighty worried about Fred. There's something awful wrong. It's up to you — like Lark Iswell says."

The sheriff studied their faces, growing bewilderment in his prominent eyes. Their real fright, almost panic, puzzled him.

"You fellers act like you was scared," he grumbled. "You don't make sense."

"We're not scared," denied Iswell. "It's the mystery that worries us. Two of our citizens have vanished without rhyme or reason and we don't like it."

Boicer gestured impatiently. "I don't give a hoot about what's happened to Sundown and Craler," he asserted. "What rowels me is *how* it happened. I want to know who done it. It wasn't Doc Smeed. He claims Sundown wasn't in the house when he got in late last night from the Ellison ranch."

"Here comes doc now," called a man. "Got Ma Simmons with him."

Dr. Smeed hurried up, a serious look on his ruddy face, his bag in hand. Mrs. Simmons walked briskly by his side, a brown-paper parcel tucked under an arm. The sheriff greeted them with a sour look.

"What's the rush, Doc?" he asked suspiciously.

"I've no time for fool questions," snapped the doctor. "If you must be curious, we've got to get out to the Ellison ranch as fast as Pablo can drive us." Dr. Smeed flung an urging look at the Mexican who said, "*Si*, — I heetch team queek." He hastened down the line of stalls, not as mystified as he might have been by the doctor's almost imperceptible wink.

Dr. Smeed lit a long black cigar, went on explaining between puffs. "You know about Raquel Perez having that heart attack. Clanton." His look shifted to the lawyer, listening intently, his lips a thin hard line. "You were out there when it happened, Iswell, In fact it was you who brought me word about it."

"How is the poor woman?" Iswell shook his head regretfully. "A terrible shock for her — seeing that Indian lying there — *murdered*."

"Dreadful business," agreed Dr. Smeed, staring at the end of his cigar. "She'll pull out of it. Mrs. Simmons is a splendid nurse."

"Why ain't you driving your own team?" queried the sheriff. He had the uneasy feeling that the doctor was deliberately snatching Pablo Casado from under his hands.

"Another fool question," retorted the doctor. "I can't run my horses day and night." He picked up his bag. "All right, Mrs. Simmons. Here's the buckboard."

He climbed in beside Pablo. Mrs. Simmons scrambled into the back seat.

"Wait a moment!" bawled the sheriff. "What about Skaggs? He's maybe layin' 'round some place, dead, and here you go, hightailin' it for the Ellison place."

Dr. Smeed frowned. "If Sundown is dead I can't do a thing for him," he pointed out. "If he's not dead it's up to you to find him." He nudged Pablo with an elbow. "Let's go — and I mean go."

Sheriff Boicer's scowling gaze followed the rapidly disappearing buckboard. He felt that something was very wrong but could not put a finger on it. His own deputy sheriff laid flat on his back with torn and bleeding feet, a badly wounded stage driver abducted, Sam Bleeker's clerk strangely missing, the Ellison's chore man murdered — hounds poisoned, and last but not least, his own and his jailer's humiliation at the hands of the elusive Ringer Barran. The baffled sheriff felt like tearing off his star and grinding it into the dust under his spurred bootheels.

Sam Bleeker broke the silence. "Ain't you goin' to do something about Fred?" he asked.

The sheriff swung on him. "Go find your own pups!" he shouted. "I got other things to do." He stamped away angrily. "Come on, boys. We've got to pick up that Barran feller's trail and do it quick."

Sam Bleeker and Tony Silver looked worriedly at Iswell. "Theesa bada beezneez," the fat saloon man muttered. "By damn, I no like."

"I'm scared," Sam admitted. "Something's happened to Fred. He wouldn't just run off." Fear was stark in the storekeeper's long face. "I'm scared enough to get away from this town."

The lawyer broke his silence. "Don't try it, Sam." His tone was deadly.

Perspiration broke on Sam Bleeker's face as he met the cold eyes of the other two men. "We've got to find Sundown," he babbled. "We've got to find him before he does any more talking about Tony."

The saloon man stared at him with wicked eyes. "By damn," he said, "you theenk theesa Fred go geeva us theesa double cross?"

"Hell, no," grunted the storekeeper. "I'll tell you what's happened to Fred. He's been nabbed — and that means the finish for the whole crowd of us."

"I think," Larkin Iswell said softly, "I think the doctor didn't tell us all he knows. In fact, I think this trip of his to the Ellison ranch is worth looking into."

"By damn yes," muttered Tony Silver. There was a greenish look to his face. "We senda for queek look one of us."

Sam Bleeker's eyes narrowed speculatively. Iswell, watching him intently, said in a thin voice, "You want the job, Sam?"

"Somebody has got to go," mumbled the storekeeper.

"It won't be you." The sneer in the lawyer's voice was plain enough.

"You don't trust me, huh?" Bleeker was shaking visibly. "Damn you, Lark!" He spoke thickly. "Damn the pair of you!" He swung on his heel. Tony Silver's huge hand fell heavily on his shoulder. "You all the beeg excite, Sam."

The soft-spoken voice held a threat that stopped the storekeeper in his tracks. He turned a ghastly look on the saloon man.

Iswell's face showed no emotion. "I'll be gone for two or three hours, Tony," he said casually.

Tony seemed to understand. He nodded. "You go for see theesa Barran?"

"He's our best bet right now," answered the lawyer.

"Sure t'ing," agreed Tony. He glanced doubtfully at Bleeker. Iswell interpreted the look. "Sam," he said, "your nerves are all shot. Why don't you go over to the hotel until I get back. Tony will give you a nice room and you can sleep it off."

"My — my store," stammered Bleeker. The lawyer interrupted him curtly. "Take him along, Tony. We know what is good for him."

"Sure t'ing," grinned the big Portuguese. "You come 'long wit' me, Sam, like gooda leetle man or maybe doc fin' you dead from bad 'eart."

Dr. Smeed might have agreed with Tony could he have seen the desperate fear in the storekeeper's eyes. He was interested in more important matters at that moment and flinging rapid-fire questions at Pablo. "I know why Kenzie smuggled Sundown away from there," he said, waving his cigar. "My fault! I shouldn't have told Tony Silver about Sundown's talk. Never dreamed there was anything to it — but go on, Pablo. I know Kenzie got Sundown away, but where has he taken him?"

Pablo's story drew approving chuckles from the doctor. He beamed over his shoulder at Mrs. Simmons. "How is that for bull luck, Ma?"

"I'm saying loud it's brains young Kenzie has got," Mrs. Simmons declared. "It was no bull luck, Doctor."

"Don't be stupid," snapped the doctor. "I mean it's luck the way my bluff worked. I didn't know where to look for Sundown, but I knew that Pablo would. That is why I told Boicer I wanted to get you out to the ranch and insisted that Pablo drive us." Dr. Smeed chuckled, lit a fresh cigar.

"Well," Mrs. Simmons said firmly, "*I'm* thinkin' it's Providence."

The old Mexican complacently tickled the buckboard team with his whip. Señora Simmons spoke true words, but it was also true that Providence had not scorned the help of a certain Pablo Casado. *Por Dios* — it was so.

CHAPTER
TWENTY

From where she stood at her balcony window Benita could look over the trees to the giant butte, rose-colored against a deep blue sky. A certain adventurous *caballero* had once paused there, and with his poniard had cut his name into the hard rock, and the date of his coming.

Benita had read those rudely-chiseled Spanish words many times. The curt statement never failed to move her.

This fourteenth day of June of the year 1639,
came Jose de Ibarra to hold the land given him
by his gracious king.

Simple words that marked the beginning of Rancho Piedra Rosa, the saga of the Ibarras. The thought thrilled Benita. She was the last living descendant of the man whose name still marked the age-weathered wall of the great butte as if defying Time or man to take what he had come to hold.

She was still confused by the startling events that had followed Rand Kenzie's return from Palo Pinto with his amazing prisoner. Benita found herself marveling at

Rand's coolness, his swift-moving efficiency. No time lost with long explanations. Within fifteen minutes she was accompanying him and Abel Gregg through the gray dawn in the light ranch wagon to the old road that lay under the high crags of Piedra Rosa Grande where Manuel Vargas waited with his huge wagons by the cold spring that trickled from the face of the cliff, the same cliff that bore witness to the coming of Jose de Ibarra more than two centuries earlier.

Sundown Skaggs, now wide awake, had grinned at her from his mattress.

"I sure was mighty puzzled," he confessed. "Couldn't figger the thing out when I come to and found myself jolting along in a wagon. Reckon I was still some fuzzy-minded. Didn't know if I was headed for Heaven or the other place. Figgered it was the other place — that doggone wagon not bein' a smooth-runnin' golden chariot. I reckon I must have let out a yell. Fust thing I knowed I was lookin' up at Chato's face and you bet that Mex hombre's face ain't no man's idee of a angel." The stage driver chuckled. "I figgered the devil had me for sure."

Sundown has said other things during the short drive back to the ranch house. "I told the doc it was Tony Silver done it. I seed Tony that in the chaparral just when he squeezed trigger. I reckon doc figgered I was ravin' plenty." Sundown's whiskered face wrinkled in a wry grin. "Cain't figger it out why Tony would want to dry gulch me thataways. Always got along fust rate with him." He finished on a puzzled note.

"We think he intended that bullet for me," Benita explained. She was sitting on the wagon floor, the old stage driver's head in her lap.

He stared up at her with outraged eyes, shook his head, strangled words in his throat. "I'm bustin' to cuss out loud," he finally muttered.

She smiled down at him. "Swear all you want to, Sundown," she had said. "I won't mind."

Raquel's voice drew the girl from the window. The old housekeeper came into the room. "You are wanted downstairs." She looked at the girl anxiously. "You are pale, my lamb."

"I'm all right," Benita asserted. "It's the — the strain." She gestured helplessly. "All these things this morning — Tom Lucky and Fred Craler locked up like prisoners in the granary, with Ace Bruff on guard — Mrs. Simmons here, nursing Sundown and Tomas. I'm wondering what will happen next."

Raquel regarded her with compassionate eyes. "The rancho has become a place of madness," she said. "It is the young señor. He is like fire that burns and destroys —" The housekeeper broke off, gave the girl an oddly wise look. "But no — I speak a lie. This young Kenzie is blessed water in a dry desert. Life will again take root and flourish on this old rancho."

"He — he is wonderful," Benita said simply.

"Ha!" The old nurse's smile was cryptic. "You are not pale any more."

The soft color in the girl's cheeks drew Rand's appreciative look, put a warmness in his eyes. Abel, from the depths of the big desk chair said mildly, "Things are movin' fast, Benita."

"I'm still in a daze." She found a seat, looked at their serious faces questioningly.

"Raquel was some peeved at us, said she wasn't goin' to have us rout you out of your nap, but Rand figgered you'd want to know."

"I wasn't sleeping," Benita said. "I'm too excited." She looked at Dr. Smeed, slumped in a chair. She had never seen such anger in him. "How are the patients?" she asked.

"Nothing wrong with 'em." The doctor scowled. "This confounded mess has me mad enough to use a gun myself."

Abel Gregg nodded sympathetically. "You tell her, Rand," he said.

"We've found out a lot that doesn't make sense — yet." Rand's tone was grim. "We know that old Tom Lucky was murdered, and the murder made to look like an accident. We know that the bullet Dr. Smeed dug out of Tomas came from Fred Craler's derringer. He's admitted it, confessed to poisoning the bounds. And Sundown claims it was Tony Silver who shot him. The events of last night prove he is not mistaken."

"Gives me the shivers," Dr. Smeed burst out. "My God, Kenzie, old Sundown would be dead now if you hadn't been a jump ahead of those damn scoundrels."

Abel saw the girl's puzzled look. "You ain't heard the facts yet," he said. "Rand and me has been so doggone busy." He gave her a brief account of the part played by Pablo Casado. "When Pablo told Rand about that talk in Iswell's back room it wasn't hard to put two and two together. Tony Silver knowed he had to close Sundown's mouth for keeps and Fred Craler was sent to do the job." Abel's eyes twinkled contentedly. "Like doc says, Rand was a jump ahead of 'em."

"It is all so maddeningly without sense," Benita said in a bewildered voice. "You say the bullet was intended for me — but why would Tony Silver want to kill *me?*" She knitted her brows at them. "And from what Pablo says, Sam, and Larkin Iswell are involved."

"I told you it didn't make sense," reminded Rand. "If we can find the right thread in the snarl of facts we'll get the right answer." He shook his head gloomily.

"You said that Tom's father was murdered," Benita went on. "What makes you think it wasn't the rock slide that killed old Tom?"

"We ain't got the straight of it yet," Abel told her. "Fred says Ringer Barran killed old Tom because Tom recognized him. Fred was in the canyon, waitin' for a chance to lay poison for the hounds. He seen the killin' and helped Barran fix the rock slide."

Benita was silent for a moment. The hideous truth was only too apparent. The poisoning of the hounds — the lurking killer. First old Tom Lucky — and then her own father. Carefully planned murder — but for what purpose? It was too confusing — a dreadful nightmare.

"I want to see Fred Craler," she said in a sharp, determined voice. "I want to see Tom. I want the truth from both of them."

212

Rand read the fear in her voice. He shook his head. "Tom had nothing to do with his father's death," he assured her.

"Tom's a no-account kid, but he wouldn't kill his own dad," Abel observed. He got out of his chair. "I'll have the boys bring 'em in."

Dr. Smeed sighed, stood up. "I'll have a look at Tomas," he said. "Sundown is over the hump, but that Navajo needs watching. Good thing we have Mrs. Simmons here." He followed Abel out to the *galeria*.

It was Benita who broke the silence. "You have had no sleep. You can't keep this up — go on and on without sleep." She looked at Rand steadily. "I have no right to let you in for all this — risk your life on my account."

He shook his head, smiled at her. "Don't let your serves get you, Benita."

"It's not fair," she insisted. "That promise to help each other was between our fathers. You are not obliged to carry out a promise your father made to mine."

"Perhaps I'm here because I want to be here," he drawled.

"You're laughing at me," flared Benita, "and — and death all around."

The twinkle left his eyes and he said soberly, "Yes, death all around us, skulking, waiting for another victim. That is why I am here, Benita, and if I seemed to be laughing it was at the thought that I should leave you to fight it alone." He was suddenly standing over her, his eyes warm on her lifted face. She gazed up at him, wordless, held in the thrall of his nearness. "I came because of that letter I found," he said huskily. "I'm staying because of you, because I —" He stopped abruptly, leaped toward the door.

There was no mistaking that sound — the reverberating crash of a rifle. Benita came out of her paralysis and ran into the *galeria*. Rand was already pushing through the gate. She sped after him, was aware of Dr. Smeed's startled face in a doorway.

She came to a halt half way across the yard, shocked gaze on the sprawled limp body of Fred Craler. She heard Abel Gregg's voice, lifted out of its usual placidity. "He must have been hidin' back of the trees, waitin' for the chance."

"Did you get a look at him?" Rand asked.

"It was awful sudden," Abel answered. "I seen Fred keel over. No, son, I didn't see who done it."

"I didn't see nothin'," Slim Purdy said. He was a lanky, red-headed youth, and the gun in his hand was leveled at Tom Lucky.

Rand's eyes questioned Ace Bruff. The cowboy shook his head. "I was close behind Fred — close enough to prod him along with my gun. He was so damn scared he could hardly drag his legs. I 'most fell on top of him when he dropped." Ace scowled at the limp form. "All I seen was smoke back of the trees. Didn't see the feller that done it."

Tom Lucky's head lifted in a look at Rand. "I know who done it." The words came from him jerkily.

"All right, Tom —" Rand studied the young Block R foreman thoughtfully. "You mean you saw him?"

Tom nodded. "Yeah — back in the trees." The foreman turned his head and looked at Benita. The shame and agony in his eyes wrung at her pity. "Yeah — I saw — Jack Fleet."

"You mean Ringer Barran," Rand said curtly.

"I wasn't knowin' he was Barran until you told me different," the foreman answered sullenly. "He told me his name was Jack Fleet."

"Do you think that shot was intended for you?" Rand flung the question sharply.

Tom widened surprised eyes at him. "He wouldn't have missed me. He don't miss his shots. I reckon it was Fred he was after all right."

Dr. Smeed came banging through the gate, bag in his hand. He glanced at the dead man. "Shot through the head," he muttered. "Didn't know what hit him." The doctor glowered. "At that the world is a better place without his kind of vermin."

Abel nodded, said mildly, "We'll 'tend to him. Doc."

Dr. Smeed's keen eyes rested for a moment on the haggard-faced foreman. What he read there seemed to hurt him. He said gruffly, not unkindly, "You young fool — don't forget they didn't come finer than that dad of yours."

"That's right," Abel said. His gaze thoughtfully followed the doctor's retreating back. "I reckon Tom ain't knowin' the story Craler give us, Rand."

"Is that right, Tom?"

The foreman seemed to stiffen under Rand's challenging look, the sharply-flung question.

"I don't savvy Abel's talk about Craler," he answered. "I never had business with Craler, except at Bleeker's store."

"You have no idea why Barran killed him?" questioned Rand.

"I never heard Jack Fleet, I mean Barran, mention Fred's name."

"I'll tell you why Barran killed Craler," Rand continued. "Craler knew the truth about your father's death."

"He was killed in that rock slide," mumbled the young foreman.

"No," Rand said. "Ringer Barran murdered him. The rock slide was faked to make you all think it was an accident. Barran didn't want you to know the truth, Tom. I don't need to tell you why."

Tom Lucky stood there like a man carved in stone, his face ashen, his eyes narrowed to pin points. He drew a long breath. "Go on, mister —" His voice was a hoarse whisper.

It was Abel Gregg who spoke. "Barran figgered to shut the kid's mouth. He was too late."

"I've got to be sure," Tom muttered thickly. "I've got to know that Craler wasn't lyin'."

"Your dad recognized him for Ringer Barran," explained Abel. He paused, brows wrinkled in deep thought. "There's plenty we ain't figgered out yet."

Ace Bruff grunted angrily. "I'm bettin' Tom can figger out why that rustler was on this range." His tone was bitter, contemptuous.

"Now Ace — don't you go makin' a bad business worse." Abel's look flickered at the dead man. "Why don't you and Slim put Craler away some place?"

Slim Purdy lowered his gun, looked uncertainly at Rand who gave him a nod. "Go ahead, Slim — we don't need you here," he said.

There was a silence while the two cowboys picked up the dead man and started toward the barn. Tom Lucky swung his head in another look at the girl. "I've been a damn skunk," he said in a choked voice. "I'm not blamin' Ace — nor any of you for thinkin' what you do about me."

She moved to him swiftly, put a hand on his arm. "Tom — it's been so hard to believe —"

"It's true, Benita," groaned the young foreman. "I had it all fixed to meet Barran at Burnt Wagon Springs tonight. He talked me into it . . . I was crazy to listen, but I did and I'm nothin' but a damn cow thief."

"Stop it!" Benita's eyes were wet. "You — you've been mad, Tom. You didn't stop to think!" She shook his arm. "Oh, if you had only stopped to think! You were born on this ranch. You have rights here that I have often thought about — since — since father died." Her voice broke.

He stared at her, jaws set tight to keep the tremble from his lips.

"Your father was part of this ranch. He put his life into it, along with my father. I had thought it all out, Tom. I wasn't forgetting you, your rights. I was planning to turn all the Lobo Mesa range over to you — for your own."

217

Tom buried his face in his hands. "My God!" he said, "I ain't worth it." His long hard body shook convulsively.

"Stop it!" she exclaimed again. "You are going to prove you *are* worth it."

Rand and Abel exchanged looks, and Rand said brusquely, "I'm riding." He turned on his heel.

Benita's voice stopped him. He looked back at her. "Riding *where?*" Her voice was tight, touched with panic.

"Well —" His quiet voice was hard steel. "It all depends which way Barran has headed."

"No!" she protested. "You mustn't —" His look silenced her, and it was Tom Lucky's voice that again halted Rand.

"I'm goin' along with you, Kenzie," he said. "Barran murdered my father. He's my meat," His shoulders straightened, and looking at him, the others saw the hard stamp of implacable resolve on his face. The weakness that had been there was gone. He spoke again, his voice resolute, yet touched with humility. "If it's all right with you." His eyes questioned them, came to rest on Rand, standing there, tall, silent, watchful.

"It's all right with me," Rand said quietly. "How about *you*, Benita?"

"Yes — yes!" She was pale, but her eyes were shining.

Abel Gregg nodded, said in his placid voice, "I reckon it's Tom's right to go along."

218

"I'll want my gun," the young foreman said simply. He went with quick, choppy strides toward the long bunkhouse under the cottonwood trees.

Abel was speaking again in his dry voice. "It's Tom's right to get the man who killed his dad and your dad," he said.

No words came from Rand Kenzie. He stood there, grave, silent, as if lost in thought. The curious expression on his stern face made Benita wonder.

CHAPTER
TWENTY-ONE

The stranger checked his house inside the gate and looked inquiringly at the two men who suddenly appeared on either side of him. He was a gaunt-framed man with a sunburned face and a drooping grizzled mustache. The eyes under the shading brim of his hat were singularly alert.

"Howdy, boys." There was a hint of ice in his voice, the shadow of a frown as he glanced at their menacing guns.

Ace Bruff looked him over carefully. "Talk some more," he finally invited. "What's your business, mister?"

The frown vanished from the rider's brown face, a smile started in the corners of his eyes, ended in a low chuckle that lifted his heavy mustache. "I reckon I left my callin' cards home, son," he answered amiably.

Slim Purdy sniggered. "No cardee, no callee . . . as solly nicee boss mans." The gun in the red-headed puncher's hand retained its steady aim.

Despite his amiable smile the stranger's eyes took on a chill look. "All right, son," he drawled, "let's say the joke is on me."

"No joke, mister." Ace waggled his gun. "If you're too bashful to tell us your business you can head back to where you come from." His voice hardened. "We ain't wastin' time jawin' with you."

The man shrugged dusty shoulders. "I want to see Abel Gregg. They told me in town I'd find him here."

The cowboys exchanged looks, and Ace said, "We ain't admittin' Abel is here. Talk some more."

For answer the horseman fumbled in a pocket and something that caught the late sunlight on its polished surface appeared in his hand.

Ace and Slim bent their heads for a closer inspection. Ace grunted, "Huh, U.S. Deputy Marshal." He lowered his gun.

"That's it," smiled the man. He studied their bronzed faces with shrewd eyes. "Trouble here, huh?"

"Plenty." Ace shoved the gun in his holster, gave the deputy marshal a mirthless grin.

"Right in our own back yard," Slim Purdy put in. "A feller cain't sashay 'cross the yard 'thout havin' to sidestep hot lead. Gets a hombre peevish."

"Sure does," agreed the deputy marshal with a grave mod.

Abel Gregg came pushing through the patio gate. Benita followed him and they stood staring at the tall man on the big brown horse. Quick recognition put a gleam in Abel's eyes. He said something to the girl, limped hurriedly toward the newcomer.

"Mighty glad to see you, Colter," he said. Vast relief was in his voice.

"Hello, Abel," The deputy marshal's look went to Benita.

"Ben's girl," Abel introduced.

Colter removed his hat, smiled gravely. "Dandled you on my knees the last time I was here," he said. "You won't be remembering me, but I was friends with your dad. before you were born." He got down from his saddle and at a nod from the girl, Slim Purdy led the horse off to the barn.

"Was it Oliphant sent you?" Abel asked.

Deputy Marshal Colter nodded. "Oliphant was tied up in court with some rustler business. He wired me at Santa Fe, asked me to pry your Palo Pinto sheriff off of Rand Kenzie's neck." Colter chuckled. "From what Oliphant says, the sheriff has Kenzie in jail on a murder charge."

"Rand wasn't stayin' in jail long," Abel said with a dry laugh.

"He wouldn't," smiled the deputy marshal.

"He left Boicer and his jailer layin' handcuffed in their own cell," chuckled Abel.

"He would," repeated Colter. His eyes twinkled. "Looks like I've wasted my time, coming all the way from Santa Fe to get him out of that jail."

Abel shook his head. "Clant Boicer is after him like a houn' dog after a b'ar. I reckon Clant is the maddest man 'tween here and the Rio Grande."

"Boicer wasn't in town when I dropped off the stage," Colter explained. "I was told you were out here so I got a horse from your barn and hit the trail for the ranch." He frowned. "Where is Kenzie now?"

"Off chasin' a killer," Abel replied.

Benita came out of her silence. She liked this steady-eyed, quiet-spoken man. "I'm awfully glad you're here," she told him earnestly. "You must come to the house and rest while we tell you about — about everything." She faltered. "It's terrible, Mr. Colter."

He gave her a compassionate look. "You've been through a lot of hell," he said. He narrowed his eyes thoughtfully at Abel. "Ben was some careless," he added. "Ben was playing with dynamite and didn't know it."

Benita widened, her eyes at him. "I don't understand." She was puzzled, startled.

"I reckon not," Colter answered gently. "It's a devil's tangle that's had us all guessin', and guessin' wrong." A grim smile lifted his grizzled mustache. "I'm putting my bets on Rand Kenzie to bust the tangle wide open. Smart of you to send for him."

"I didn't," Benita said.

"Huh?" The deputy marshal was surprised.

"It was a letter Ben wrote to Jeff Kenzie," explained Abel. "Ben wasn't knowin' that Jeff was dead. Rand found the letter and come on the jump." He smiled dryly. "Landed square in Boicer's jail."

Benita repeated her invitation. "We can only wait until Rand gets back — and perhaps you might like a drink."

"Swallowed some dust coming over Sand Crawl," admitted Colter. "A drink'll go down fine."

The deputy marshal was not to have his refreshment, at least not just then. A shout from Ace Bruff checked them at the garden gate.

"Kenzie comin'!" be yelled.

Benita glimpsed Rand, his big buckskin stepping daintily through the trees beyond the corral fence. Another buckskin, amazingly like Mingo, only smaller, trailed at the end of a lead-rope, with something that sagged across the saddle. A second rider appeared, Tom Lucky, his tall frame curiously slumped forward.

Ace and Slim went pounding across the yard toward the back gate. Abel Gregg grunted excitedly, started after them, Benita at his heels.

The deputy marshal took a quick step, halted, stared intently at a cloud of dust lifting in the distance and approaching rapidly. He turned to follow the others, his eyes narrowed thoughtfully.

Benita's swifter feet carried her past the limping old man. She came to a breathless standstill, eyes big on Rand as he rode into the yard. Her look slid past him, to the thing lashed to the smaller buckskin, and then rested on Tom Lucky. She uttered a frightened cry, ran to the side of his horse and caught his sagging weight in her arms. Ace Bruff sprang to her aid and between there they lifted the young foreman from his saddle.

He forced a tight-lipped smile. "I'm all right." He leaned heavily on the stocky cowboy. "Lost some blood."

Rand swung from his saddle, spoke tersely to Slim Purdy. The cowboy said, "Sure." and started away on the run.

"I sent him for the doctor," Rand said as he hurried over to Benita, standing with an arm around the wounded foreman.

224

Her look went briefly to the body lashed to the buckskin mare. Rand nodded, said curtly. "Yes — that's Barran. Tom got him."

Abel Gregg limped up, gazed at the dead outlaw. He shook his head regretfully. "Would have looked better dangling at the end of a rope," he grumbled.

"Barran wasn't the kind to give up without a fight," Rand said.

"Tough hombre, huh?" grunted Abel. "Yeah, I reckon he'd plenty guts. Only trouble with Barran was he took the wrong trail. That's the doggone truth about *him*." His gaze shifted questioningly to Tom Lucky. "Hurt bad, young feller?"

"I'm all right," the foreman repeated. He forced another smile. "Barran's bullet smashed my arm — but I got him. He won't do any more killin'."

They looked at him in silent understanding. There was a strength in his face that had not been there before, a new and resolute light in his eyes.

It was Benita who spoke. "I'm glad, Tom. Oh, so glad." Her grave little smile was a benediction. They knew what she meant — that she was thinking of Tom Lucky's new-found manhood.

Deputy Marshal Colter's drawling voice drew their eyes. "Looks like you're right busy these days, Rand." His gaze slid over the body lashed to the buckskin mare, and back to Rand. "Don't see why Oliphant had me chasing all the way from Santa Fe to get you out of a jam. You ain't needin' my help, young feller, or —" His look shifted to the half score riders swinging into the avenue from the road. "Or am. I wrong?" he finished softly.

"I've an idea you're wrong," Rand answered with a wry grin. "If my eyes don't deceive me that's my friend the sheriff and it looks as if he's caught up with me this time."

Benita gasped. "He'll kill you! He told me he would shoot on sight!" She went swiftly to Rand, as if she would shield him from the guns in the hands of the approaching horsemen. The press of her body against him drew his eyes in a look that ran through her like fire. He said in a low voice, "It's all right, it's all right."

Boicer and his posse roared up in a cloud of dust. The sheriff's eyes went to Rand as if drawn by a magnet. His voice lifted in an exultant shout. "It's Barran, fellers! We've got the skunk penned this time."

Rand met his triumphant gaze with a cool smile. "You're too late, Boicer. We've already got Ringer Barran."

The sheriff's gun menaced him. "You're some mixed up," he jibed. "You may be Kenzie to some fools you can bluff, but to me you're Ringer Barran and you're sure headed back to jail — and a hangman's rope." He slid from his saddle. "Keep him covered, boys. I'm tying him up my own self."

"One moment, Sheriff —" The lazy drawl was gone from Colter's voice. "You've treed the wrong bear. I happen to know that this man is Rand Kenzie — a good friend of mine."

Boicer eyed him truculently. "Who in the hell are you?" he demanded.

226

Colter silently held out his silver badge. Boicer stared at it, lifted surprised eyes to the deputy marshal's impassive face. One of the riders said softly, "That badge don't lie, Clant. I know Ed Colter — and that's him."

"I'll be damned," muttered the sheriff. His disappointed gaze went to Rand. "So you *are* Kenzie?"

"That's right," confirmed Rand. He was staring with curiously intent eyes at the sheriff's saddle.

The sheriff was remembering the indignities he had suffered in his own jail. He began to splutter angry words. He broke off, stared with bulging eyes at the lifeless body roped to the buckskin mare. His jaw sagged.

"Rand was just tellin' you we'd got Ringer Barran," Abel said dryly. "You was claimin' the killer of Ben Ellison was forkin' a buckskin." Satisfaction put a gleam in Abel's eyes. "Well — there's your buckskin, Clant, and that dead man is your Ringer Barran."

Boicer seemed to be having difficulty with his tongue. He mumbled something, moved close to the mare, stood gazing at the dead outlaw. The posse pushed their horses up for a near view.

"No brand on that buckskin," one of the riders commented.

"Sure there ain't," agreed Abel. "Ringer Barran caught that mare up from the wild bunch. She's a double for Kenzie's buckskin if she was bigger."

Boicer's head turned in a look at Rand. The animosity had gone from his eyes, and there was a relaxed look to him, as though a vexing problem had been forever solved. "I was right, and I was wrong," he said with a wide grin. "Wrong about you, but right about Ben Ellison's murderer ridin' a buckskin." The sheriff's voice oozed with satisfaction. "I reckon that closes the case, and no hard feelin's, Kenzie. You've no call to blame me for throwin' you in jail like I done. I couldn't do nothin' else under the circumstances."

"You say the case is closed, Boicer?" Rand's quiet voice held a hint of steel, and again. Benita wondered at the curious expression that flickered across his face.

"Hell, yes," asserted the sheriff irritably. "I don't know how you boys done it, but there ain't no doubt but what you got the man that killed Ben Ellison." He broke off, looked inquiringly at Dr. Smeed as the latter hurried up.

"More dead men," grumbled the doctor with a brief glance at the buckskin's grim burden. "Well, my boy, let's have a look at that arm." He turned with professional interest to the Block R foreman, flung terse words back at the sheriff as he removed the makeshift bandage. "Too bad you didn't get here sooner, Clanton. You'd have saved Craler's life. Not that it matters a hoot. Craler was a born killer and Barran's bullet did a good job when it put an end to him."

"Huh?" Boicer was startled. "Fred Craler — *dead?*"

He listened with growing amazement to Abel's laconic account of Rand's activities the previous night.

"Beats the devil," he muttered. "So you've got old Sundown hid out here." He shook his head. "Don't make sense."

228

Dr. Smeed looked round at him impatiently. "Use your head, Clant. It's as plain as the nose on your face. Tony Silver took a shot at Benita but hit Sundown instead. Sundown recognized Tony in the chaparral. I thought he was raving and told Tony as a joke, and that was Sundown's death warrant."

"It don't make sense," repeated the bewildered sheriff. "Tony Silver's a good citizen."

"Don't be a fool," exploded Dr. Smeed. "Tony and Iswell and Bleeker are all mixed up in the business. They sent Craler over to my house last night to kill Sundown to keep him from talking. Rand Kenzie was too smart for them. Now you get busy and arrest those scoundrels before they do some more killing." The doctor returned his attention to the wounded arm. "All right, Tom. Let's get to the house. No sense working on you out here."

The foreman reluctantly allowed himself to be led away. The sheriff's puzzled look followed him. "How did he get shot?" he asked. "I didn't know Tom was hurt."

"Barran wasn't the man to be taken alive," Abel Gregg answered. "Figger it out for yourself, Clant." He added grimly, "The doc was handin' you some good advice. You should head back to town and slap them fellers in jail."

"All I've had is a lot of crazy talk," complained the sheriff angrily. "Why in hell should Tony Silver want to kill Benita?" His shocked gaze went to the girl.

She shook her head, lifted her face in an appealing look at Rand who said softly, "Why don't you find out, Boicer?"

The sheriff's eyes narrowed. "You mean they're maybe mixed up with Ben Ellison's murder?" His tone was thoughtful.

"I'm not saying," retorted Rand. "We do know it was Tony who ambushed the stage, and we know they sent Craler to kill Sundown, and that it was Craler who poisoned the hounds and shot Tomas." Rand's voice hardened. "We know something else, Boicer."

"Huh?" The sheriff was visibly jolted. He stiffened and his eyes took on a wary look.

"It was no accident that killed old Tom Lucky," Rand continued. "It was murder, and Ringer Barran was the murderer."

The sheriff showed relief. "That don't surprise me," he said with a grating laugh. "I reckon that's why he killed Ben Ellison. Ben was on to him." He gestured impatiently. "Let's go, boys. One of you put a lead-rope on that mare. We'll take Barran back to town with us." His laugh grated again. "Wouldn't be right, leavin' him lay on *this* ranch."

Abel Gregg said mildly, "Take Craier along with you, Clant. Red Rock Ranch ain't got ground for him, I'm thinkin'."

"Sure," asserted the sheriff. He added sourly, "I'm needin' more evidence before I go throwing Tony Silver and the others in jail."

The deputy marshal broke his silence. "I'm kind of interested in this Tony Silver," he said in his drawling voice. "Portuguese, ain't he? A big fat feller . . . laughs hearty . . . a slap-you-on-the-back hombre."

"That's him," grunted the sheriff.

Colter felt inside a pocket, extracted a large brown envelope from which he selected a small photograph. "Would this look like him?"

Boicer studied the picture. He nodded, said in a surprised voice, "That's Tony . . . sure it's Tony."

Colter produced two more small pictures. The sheriff gaped at them. "Larkin Iswell," he said in a startled voice. "Sam Bleeker — but hell — them's convict pictures."

The deputy marshal carefully returned the pictures to the brown envelope. "Yeah," he drawled, "convict pictures, Boicer. That's why I'm interested."

"Can you beat it?" marveled the sheriff. "Them fellers have been in Palo Pinto five or six years. Bleeker owns the store. He's makin' good money, and so is Tony. He's rich, owns the hotel and the Palace Bar . . . he's pardners with Lark Iswell in the money-lendin' business."

"Nice honest citizens," murmured Colter. He stared fixedly at the sheriff. "You never suspected anything wrong about 'em, Boicer?"

"You cain't drag *me* into it!" Boicer glared wrathfully. "I've been sheriff only some six months."

"Ben Ellison took more interest in them," the deputy marshal drawled. "I reckon that's why he had to die."

The sheriff thought it over for a moment. "Yeah," he agreed in a stifled voice. "They'd want to kill him — he was on to 'em."

Abel grunted impatiently. "Seems like we're wastin' time," he grumbled. "Let's head for town pronto. I crave to see that damn outfit in the calaboose."

Colter saw the girl's bewilderment. He said gently, "It's like this, Benita — your dad suspected there was something wrong with Bleeker and Silver. He didn't suspect Larkin Iswell was one of them, but something he'd heard gave him the idea that Bleeker and Silver were escaped convicts. He got in touch with me and I wrote to him for more information." Colter shook his head regretfully. "I didn't know that Bleeker is postmaster. He must have opened my letter to Ben and I guess it was Ben's death warrant."

"I reckon that's the story," muttered Abel. "You've got it figgered right, Ed."

Rand was silent, his brooding gaze fixed on the sheriff.

Abel spoke again, his voice perplexed. "Where does Iswell get into the picture, Ed? You say Ben wasn't suspecting Lark Iswell. Seems to me Lark would have kept out of it."

"Iswell was the brains," Colter replied. He smiled grimly. "Was ain't quite the word. He's still on the job." He paused, added thoughtfully, "Iswell had to play the hand out. The trail was getting too hot. He saw to it that Ben couldn't do any more talking. There was one thing he didn't know. Ben was worried because he didn't hear from me." Colter frowned. "At least that's my notion. Ben must have done some hard thinking and realized that Bleeker had held up my letter. He wrote again, posted the letter in Las Cruces. He told me not to write him at the Palo Pinto post office."

"You was a long time gettin' here, Ed," fumed Abel.

232

"I was away, down in Mexico," explained Colter. "I found Ben's letter — and Oliphant's wire — when I got back to Santa Fe. I caught the first stage out."

Benita stole a glance at Rand. His face was a cold, unrevealing mask. She said hesitantly to Colter, "There is so much that doesn't quite fit. Where does Ringer Barran come in? Why did Tony Silver want to kill me?" She faltered, added slowly, "I — I think we haven't found *all* the answers yet, Mr. Colter."

Sheriff Boicer stared at her. "Ain't no other answers, Benita," he said. "Ed Colter ain't missed a bet and I'm saying out loud we've got the mystery licked." His heavy voice took on a tender note. "You go back to the house and leave things to me. I'll take care of them wolves."

Benita hesitated, said bluntly, "I'm not satisfied. I want to know why Ringer Barran killed old Tom Lucky, and my father, and I want to know why Tony Silver tried to kill *me*." She stopped abruptly, disturbingly aware of the press of Rand's hard-muscled arm against her shoulder. She heard his quiet voice.

"Tony was afraid your father had told you about that letter," Rand said. "Tony wanted to make sure there was nobody left to talk."

"You've got it!" exclaimed Abel.

Rand continued quietly, "Of course it would be Iswell's idea. With Ben Ellison out of the way, and anybody else who might know the truth, it would be easy for Iswell to forge a letter in Ben Ellison's handwriting, a letter to Ed Colter, telling him the whole thing was a mistake." Rand looked inquiringly at the deputy marshal.

Colter nodded, "I got that letter," he drawled. "Ben wrote me to drop the matter, said he'd made a mistake."

"It was a forged letter," Rand declared. "It must have been."

"Of course it was forged." Colter's tone was bleak. "You see, there was a date on that letter. It was mailed out of Palo Pinto the night after Ben was killed. That's the odd thing about it. Why would Iswell send me that forged letter *after* Ben was dead?"

It was Rand who broke the stunned silence. "It's possible Iswell didn't know Ben Ellison was dead when he sent that letter," he said softly.

"Meanin' what?" demanded the sheriff irritably. He went on, not waiting for an answer. "Easy enough to figger the thing out. Lark Iswell wouldn't know how quick Ringer Barran would get at Ben. He went to work and sent off that letter before Barran had time to let him know he'd done the job."

"If Oliphant hadn't sent me the wire to mosey over here and haul you off of Kenzie's neck I maybe wouldn't be here now," Colter said ruefully. "You see, Iswell was serving time for forgery when he broke loose. Tony Silver was doing a life term for a lot of murders. Bleeker was just a cheap insurance-collectin' arsonist."

Benita's mind was in a whirl. She was seeing Larkin Iswell again, his narrow, pointed face, his sly smile. It seemed years since she had sat there with him in the

234

galeria only the day before. She had realized then that the note was a forgery, not because of the handwriting. She could have sworn the handwriting was her father's. Iswell's blunder alone had betrayed the forgery.

Cold prickles chased up and down her spine. She understood now. Her death would have placed the stamp of authenticity on that note. Nobody could have disputed its genuineness. Larkin Iswell's claim would have stood in law and he would have become the owner of Red Rock Ranch. His offer of marriage was only a blind. He would not have stopped at another murder.

The deputy marshal was speaking again. "It wasn't until I got to Las Cruces and was talking with a man there that I realized Ben couldn't have written that letter. He was already dead."

"Lark must be a slick hand with the pen, all right," muttered the sheriff. He climbed into his saddle. "All right, boys. Let's go."

"We'll ride with you, Boicer," Rand said.

"Ain't needing your help," the sheriff answered gruffly. "I can handle this business, Kenzie. You keep out of it."

The posse drifted out of the yard. Colter looked curiously at Rand's set face. "You mean that — about going to town?" he asked.

"It's necessary," Rand answered. "*Very* necessary."

The deputy marshal's keen eyes took on a steely glint. "I'll go along with you," he said simply.

Rand nodded, spoke briefly with Ace Bruff. The cowboy narrowed thoughtful eyes. "Sure," he said. "We ain't awful chummy with Rafter B but I reckon Slim and me can pull it off." He vanished into the barn.

Abel Gregg's shrewd eyes followed him. He beckoned to Pablo Casado. "Get the team hitched," he told the Mexican. "We're headin' for town."

Misgivings seized Benita. She sensed that the dreadful affair was not finished. The implacable mask that was Rand Kenzie's face frightened her. He knew it was not finished — was going to Palo Pinto to finish it. She wanted to cry out to him, beg him not to go. The look of hard resolve in his eyes held her tongue-tied. She turned, made her way blindly down the yard. Raquel was watching from the patio gate. The old nurse ran to her.

"You look so afraid," she exclaimed in a concerned voice.

"I am," Benita said huskily. "Oh, Raquel — when will it end?"

CHAPTER
TWENTY-TWO

The sound of horsemen approaching up the street lifted Larkin Iswell from his chair. With a swift movement of his hand be lowered the lamp wick and blew out the light.

His hat lay on the desk. He put it on, went to the window and stood watching the riders straggle past. The moon, already low to the western hills gave enough light for the lawyer to distinguish Sheriff Boicer's bulky figure in the lead.

His lips twisted in a thin smile. He stepped through the door, pulled it shut cautiously and started up the board sidewalk toward the hotel.

The crowd in front of the hotel was a magnet that drew the sheriff and his posse to a standstill. Boicer flung himself from his saddle, the light of the flaring kerosene lamp full on his face.

"What's wrong here?" His loud, arrogant voice put a hush on them. Faces turned toward him, and after a moment a voice said, "Sam Bleeker has killed himself, Clant."

Boicer's hand was on his holstered gun and he said softly, "Yeah?" His look went briefly to the riders at his back and there was a scraping of saddle leathers, the quick stamp of feet as the men swung down. They gathered around the sheriff, guns in their hands.

The sheriff spoke again, brusquely, "Where's Tony?"

"He's up there with Sam," the same voice answered. The speaker pushed through the crowd, showed the frightened face of the desk clerk. "We just found Sam layin' there, dead. He shot himself."

Before the sheriff could reply another voice broke in. "It's a doggone mess, Clant." Shorty Tod's worried face appeared under the lamplight. "Sam ain't been 'round all day and I cain't get the mail bags. It's awful serious business, holdin' up the U.S. mail."

"Ain't your fault, Shorty," the sheriff said. "If the postmaster goes and kills himself the gove'ment ain't going to jump on *your* neck."

"It's got me crazy," grumbled Shorty Tod. "I've been holdin' the stage all day. Cain't pull out an' not have the U.S. mail on board. Sure wish Sundown hadn't gone and hid hisself. I'm buffaloed."

Another voice lifted, a bellowing shout from the lobby. "By damn, Clant . . . beega trouble . . . Sam — he go keela 'eemself, you bet."

Tony Silver ploughed through the bystanders. The lamplight caught the shine of perspiration on his olive-skinned face. He held up a sheet of paper in his hand. "Sam leeva thees note by damn!"

"Huh?" The sheriff's tone was thoughtful. "Let's have a look at that note, Tony."

Larkin Iswell was suddenly a vague motionless shape in the darkness. He stood, rigid, eyes focused on the sheriff's face under the glare of the overhead lamp. He

238

heard Shorty Tod's aggrieved voice. "You're the law, Clant. You should go into the store an' turn them mail bags over to me."

Boicer shook his head impatiently. "Listen," he said gruffly. "What Sam says here in this note explains plenty. Sam says Sundown Skaggs had found out he'd been stealin' from the gove'ment. Sam was scared, sent a feller to get Sundown up in Piñon Pass, and when Sundown wasn't killed he sent Fred Craler over to doc's house to finish him. Sundown got away, which is why Sam figgered a bullet in his own head was the best way out."

Something in the sheriff's voice seemed to disturb the lawyer. He shrank closer to the deeper darkness of the alley. The sheriff was speaking again, his voice heavy skepticism. "You say Sam left this note, Tony?"

"Sure t'ing," asserted the saloon man. "Sam acts queer theesa morning because Fred no show up at store. Sam he tella me he seek man, want room for getta sleep. He go sleep all day. No answer knock, so I go for see and finda Sam dead . . . finda theesa note he leave."

"Makes a good story, Tony," chortled the sheriff. "Are you sure you ain't lyin'? Wasn't it Lark Iswell who give you this note?"

Iswell's shocked eyes saw a strange thing. He saw the sheriff's hand lift, and two men were suddenly pressing guns hard against Tony's ribs. The lawyer roused from his paralysis, melted into the darkness of the alley. He came to an abrupt standstill, stared at the two vague shapes that drifted in front of him. He felt the prod of steel against his side, heard Rand Kenzie's bleak voice. "Take him to the barn, Ace."

Another shape materialized from the darkness, and a voice said grimly, "That's him — that's the feller." The deputy marshal followed Rand into the street.

Abel Gregg slid up on Indian-quiet feet. "Clant has jumped Tony," he told them. His frowning gaze was fixed up-street on the crowd milling under the glare of the kerosene lamp. "Sam Bleeker has killed himself. I heard the talk, saw Lark Iswell take a sneak into the alley."

"He sneaked right into our arms," Rand told him laconically.

Boicer swept the three men with a triumphant look as they halted inside the circle of lamplight. "I wasn't needing your help," he said. "I've got Tony, and I've got him proper."

Tony glared at him murderously. He stood quietly enough between the two men whose guns pressed against his huge body, his face the color of dirty tallow and beaded with perspiration. "By damn, you 'ave go crrazy," he spluttered.

"I reckon not, Tony," smiled the sheriff. "You had the town fooled for a long time, you and Bleeker and Iswell." The sheriff laughed stridently. "You've played the string out, Tony."

Tony seemed to shrink visibly. His look played around with the desperation of a trapped animal. His huge arms jerked up like steel flails that sent the two deputies reeling back into the circle of bystanders. In an instant a gun was in his hand.

240

The appalled sheriff gaped at him. Tony's eyes were glints of death in their folds of flesh. He crouched behind the terrified desk clerk, gun menacing them.

"I keel any man who try stoppa me," he said. He continued to back toward the lobby door, pulling the desk clerk along with one huge hand.

They watched, silent, helpless. They dared not shoot for fear of killing the unfortunate clerk. Rand's voice broke the tense silence.

"You can't get away, Tony," he said. "Not through *that* door. You're trapped."

Tony's head turned in a startled look behind him and in that unguarded instant smoke and flame poured from Rand's gun. Tony lurched sideways under the impact of the heavy bullet, tripped on the lower porch step and sprawled his length.

The deputies were on him in a moment. They jerked him to his feet.

"Smashed his arm," one of them said. He threw Rand an admiring look. "Some shootin', mister."

Sheriff Boicer wiped his hot face, grinned at Rand. "Thanks, Kenzie. Kind of squares that play you pulled off at the jail."

Ed Colter interrupted him. "What is this talk about Sam Bleeker?" he asked curtly.

"Sam's killed himself," answered the sheriff. "He's layin' upstairs some place." His tone was arrogant again. "Sam will keep. I've got more important things to do right now. This job ain't finished until I get Lark Iswell in jail."

"Iswell is already under arrest," the deputy marshal told him coldly. "How do you know Bleeker killed himself, Boicer?"

The sheriff held up the crumpled sheet of paper still clutched in his fingers. "He left this note, or Tony claims he did." He grinned at the prisoner. "It's my notion that Lark Iswell wrote it."

"You mean it's not suicide?" Colter nodded. "I think you're right, Sheriff."

"Murder," grunted the sheriff. "Iswell fixed up the note to make it look like suicide. It means the rope for both of 'em, Tony *and* Lark."

"We nabbed Iswell in the alley," Colter told him. "We've got him over at the barn."

"Yeah?" Boicer spoke angrily. "Seems to me you're actin' kind of smart in my county, Colter. *You* ain't got the right to go arrestin' Lark Iswell. I'm sheriff here and Iswell is my prisoner."

The deputy marshal hesitated, glanced at Rand who nodded. Colter suddenly laughed. "All right, Boicer," he drawled. "Come on over to the barn if you want Iswell."

"You bet I'll come," blustered the sheriff. "Iswell's *my* prisoner." He looked at Tony Silver, dejected, terrified, the fight gone out of him. "Take him over to the jail, some of you boys. The rest of you come along with me."

Slim Purdy stood in the lighted entrance of the big livery barn. He gave Rand a knowing grin as the men trooped up, a grin that tightened to a hard grimace as he saw the sheriff.

242

"Where's Iswell at?" were the sheriff's first words. He stepped through the door, stared about suspiciously, looking for the prisoner.

Slim answered nonchalantly, "Ace has him back in the barn some place."

Boicer showed relief. "We'll take him over to the jail," he said. A wide smile spread across his face. "I reckon this county will sure hand it to me for cleanin' up a bunch of killers, including the man who murdered Ben Ellison." The sheriff's look went resentfully to Rand. "I'd have taken Ringer Barran alive if you hadn't pushed your nose into my business. I wanted to see Ben's killer swing."

"Don't worry, Boicer." Rand spoke softly. "Ben Ellison's murderer is going to hang. You have my promise."

"Huh?" Boicer stiffened, stared at Rand intently, "Barran is dead. No sense hangin' a dead man."

Rand shook his head. "Barran didn't kill Ellison," he said. "You see, Boicer, the murderer of Ben Ellison is still alive." Rand's gun whipped up, covered the dumbfounded sheriff. His voice hardened. "Don't move, Boicer."

There was a stir behind the sheriff as the possemen reached for their guns. Abel Gregg's dry voice held them in check.

"Don't try it, boys," he warned. "No sense dyin' for a killin' skunk like him."

"We don't get you," muttered one of the deputies. "You're arrestin' our sheriff . . . claiming he killed Ellison."

"You sure get the truth quick," chuckled Abel.

Boicer's face was ghastly. He made no protest when the deputy marshal deftly handcuffed him, and looking at him, the possemen's faces hardened. They were honest citizens, deputized by their sheriff to hunt down the murderer of a man they had respected and liked. They felt outraged and puzzled. The thing was unbelievable, but the guilt stark on Boicer's face left no room for doubt.

The deputy marshal read their perplexed thoughts. He said quietly, "I'll turn him over to you men. You know who I am, and I'm warning you to hold him safe for trial."

"You bet we'll hold him," growled one of the deputies. "He won't have a chance to bust jail."

Boicer broke his silence. "You're all crazy," he gasped. "You ain't got proof."

Two shapes emerged from one of the stalls. Boicer's prominent eyes bulged as he recognized the man with Ace Bruff.

Bert Ketcher gave him a sullen look. "Yeah," he said, "I talked . . . talked plenty."

"You damn fool!" shouted Boicer.

"I wasn't fool enough to let you leave me holdin' the bag," retorted Ketcher. "I had it straight from Ace Bruff an' Slim Purdy about how you figgered to frame me." Ketcher broke off as he saw the hard grin on Ace Bruff's face. He turned pale, shifted shocked eyes to the dazed sheriff.

Rand said quietly, "You fell for the bait, Ketcher — but it's too late now."

244

One of the deputies spoke, an elderly, grizzled cowman. "How come you fellers figgered it was Clant who killed Ben Ellison?" He looked inquiringly at Abel.

Rand answered the question. "It's a badly mixed-up business, with Boicer playing his game and Iswell's gang playing theirs. Neither side knew the other was involved. Iswell had to kill Ellison because Ellison had guessed the truth — that he and Bleeker and Silver were escaped convicts. Iswell hired Ringer Barran to kill Ellison. Barran did kill Tom Lucky because Tom recognized him although he was wearing the name of Jack Fleet. He didn't kill Ben Ellison."

"How do you know he didn't?" queried the same deputy.

"Ben Ellison was killed with a shotgun," Rand said. "Barran didn't carry a shotgun." He paused, looked grimly at the sheriff. "Boicer does. You all know he carries a shotgun in his saddle boot."

"Clant was some partial to a shotgun," agreed the grizzled cowman. "Yeah, he always carried a shotgun 'round with him." He shook his head doubtfully. "Why would Clant want to kill Ben?"

"Boicer was secretly working with a gang of rustlers," explained Rand. "He was receiving stolen cattle, holding them on his Rafter B. He got himself elected sheriff as a blind. Ben Ellison found out the truth. Boicer knew he was finished, went out to Ellison's place and emptied his shotgun into him." Rand swung savagely on Bert Ketcher. "That's right, isn't it? We have your signed confession."

"That's right," Ketcher mumbled. He stared down sullenly at his bandaged feet.

Slim Purdy grinned at the others. "Couldn't get his boots on him. His feet is swelled up too bad."

"You're a devil," Ketcher muttered, looking up at Rand.

Rand smiled grimly. "You won't swing with Boicer," he said to Ketcher. "You weren't mixed up in *that* business. There's a chance we'll turn you loose when you've done your talking in court."

"Providin' he gets out of this part of the country," muttered the grizzled cowman.

"Boicer put on a good act," continued Rand. "He had to catch a murderer. He'd heard about a mysterious lone rider on a buckskin seen in the hills. It made good talk and when I came along on my buckskin horse he slapped me in jail. It would have closed the case to convict me as the killer. And then Larkin Iswell stepped in. He really believed that Ringer Barran *had* killed Ellison. He never dreamed that Boicer was the murderer, but it suited him to have somebody caught and hung, or otherwise eliminated. To make it a certainty he came with a plan to break me out of jail. If I had gone through that window I would have been shot as Ringer Barran. In fact it was Iswell who put it into Boicer's head that I was Barran. The murder of Ben Ellison would have been a closed chapter."

"It's sure closed now," Abel Gregg said dryly. His voice lifted. "Pablo — fetch that coyote you've got back there in the stall."

246

The Mexican appeared, pushing Iswell in front of him at the point of his big *machete*. "Thees no coyote," he said. "Thees theeng just r-rattlesnik." He shoved the lawyer into the hard hands of the glowering deputies.

U.S. Deputy Marshal Colter gave him an ironical smile. "Looks like I'm cheated out of the pleasure of taking you back to the pen, Iswell," he drawled. "Kenzie's fixed things so you'll have to stay here in Palo Pinto until they hang you, alongside of Tony Silver and Boicer."

CHAPTER
TWENTY-THREE

They halted their horses in the shadow of the lofty red butte. Rand drew out tobacco and papers and Benita watched in silence while his strong brown fingers shaped the cigarette. He lit it, smiled down at her through a thin haze of blue smoke.

She gestured. "Don Jose Ibarra passed this way a long, long time ago," she said. "I wanted you to see the inscription he cut in the rock. Such brave words. They remind me of you."

Her nearness, the sound of her voice, stirred him. He pinched out the cigarette, tossed it aside. "You're sweet," he said huskily, "sweet, and fine — and adorable."

She kept her eyes away from him, sat there in the saddle, slim and lovely, a new radiance in her.

"I want to ask you something —" She spoke with visible effort, as though reluctant to bring up a distasteful subject. "It's about Clanton Boicer. When did you first suspect him?"

"Well —" Rand pondered a moment. "It was the shotgun. You see, it was when Boicer cornered me in the yard yesterday that I first noticed the shotgun in his saddle boot."

"I saw you looking at his horse," Benita remembered. "I wondered —" She broke off.

"I knew it couldn't have been Ringer Barran," Rand continued. "Barran was not the man to use a shotgun. He didn't have one, but Boicer did. A sawed-off shotgun. He always had it with him in his saddle boot, I learned, and the shells he used were loaded with buckshot."

The girl shivered, and he said harshly, "Let's forget it! It's over with."

Benita shook her head. "I want to know —"

"It was the motive that bothered me," Rand went on reluctantly. "The shotgun was enough to raise my suspicions, but I was stumped for a motive. And then I got an idea — sent Ace and Slim to Rafter B —"

"I saw you talking to Ace," she again remembered.

"Well, it worked," Rand said grimly. "Bert Ketcher supplied the missing motive." He paused, added gently, "It's all done with — forever. Put it behind you, Benita."

"Yes," she said in a voice hardly audible. "We'll put it behind us. It is what father would say."

They got down from their saddles, and Rand stood gazing at the words so bravely cut in the hard face of the butte.

This fourteenth day of June of the year 1639, came Jose de Ibarra to hold the land given him by his gracious king.

"A long time ago," Benita said when he looked at her. Her voice was low, touched with something that filled his eyes with a warm look. "You came only a few days ago — and so much has happened."

His arms went out to her, and she felt the strength of them draw her close. She only smiled, her face lifted to his, her eyes very tender.

"Yes," Rand said, quietly, confidently, "and like Jose de Ibarra I will hold what is mine."

The big buckskin horse cocked interested ears at the two figures standing so close in the shadow of the great red butte. It was none of his business. He switched his tail, fell to nibbling the bunch grass.